Monster

EARL MOORE

Earl Moore

This is a book of fiction. Any references or similarities to actual events, real people, or real locations are intended to give the novel a sense of reality. Any similarity to other names, characters, places and incidents are entirely coincidental.

ISBN: 9798737466985

Book Production: Crystell Publications
Cover Design – Crystell Publications
E-Mail – minkassitant@yahoo.com
(405) 414-3991

Printed in the USA

Monster

PROLOGUE

OF THINGS PAST

"'...Yeah, my bad, Monster, that was Day Day on my other line."

"Shit, don't worry about it, nigga. What he talkin' about anyway?" Monster asked.

"A nigga just wanna know what's crackin' wit getting them niggas back. So what's good, but? It's going down or what, Monster?" Geno asked ready for action.

"Yeah, yeah, but, we got it. We got it, Geno. How many thangs you got?" Monster questioned.

"Shit, umm..." Geno thought for a second, trying to calculate quickly. "I got two Glock nines, three AKs, a couple of shottys and I just copped this mini Mac ten from a nigga. Plus I got four vests, masks, and gloves, nigga, Geno finished proudly.

"Damn!" Monster started, "what, you startin' a fuckin' army, young bull?"

"Aww, young but, ya know a nigga gots to stay strapped," Geno replied with emphasis.

"check this out. I think we got enough off of your stock alone. Ay, but look, tell Day Day to get ready, start movin' niggas around. It's 'bout to be a wipeout. Niggas done forgot who da fuck Monster is, Yo I might start jogging niggas memory off g.p. now!" exclaimed Monster angrily.

"No doubt, nigga. Ay, let's get... oh, who da fuck?!"

"What, nigga? You Alright, Geno?"

"Hold on, Monster, hold on... its some niggas..."

"Geno?! "

"Yeah, nigga, I "fin bout to fuck niggas... "CLACK CLACK" ... up, Monster.

Niggas is crazy for comin' here!" Geno called out with venom dripping in his tone"Geno, what the fuck is going on, nigga?!" Monster asked, hysterical about his nigga. He didn't know what was going on until he'd heard it. He knew Geno had cocked a gun on the other end... but for what? he thought to himself. Then, in an instant, he realized what was going on once he heard the gun blasts through the phone's receiver.

'BOOM BOOM!' The shots from a semi auto rang out alongside the. retort from what was clearly an automatic weapon, 'TAT TAT TOW!'

"Ow...shit!" Monster could hear Geno through the receiver.

He must have dropped it, Monster thought to himself. "Ay, G, pick up the phone, nigga!" Then. he heard Geno again.

"Ay, what you Join' here? Man, don't..." 'BOOM BOOM BOOM!' Those were the last sounds that Monster heard on his end. Period.

CHAPTER 1

INTRODUCTION

Monster and Geno sat at the table while Day Day and Bone Neck stood watch over their two friends. Everybody was a little nervous because they had never done business with these niggas before. There were about ten people in the small condo that hadn't come with Monster, Geno, Day Day and Bone Neck; the key players on 7th Street.

Monster, or Earl Moore, is the head nigga in charge and brains behind the millions that flow because of their drug market and reign of terror they could bring any clique in the way. At 23, He'd been in the game since he was 13 years old. He was also about fifteen minutes away from take off in the rap industry. He earned the title "Monster" simply. He was just that to the streets. A damn Monster. He was the leader in money, stature, and intellect.

He'd made a pact that he wouldn't retire until his income and savings. topped 3, tripled, three times, in three sets of numerical columns. In other words, His goal was to reach $999,999,999. Or 9 nines. He wanted to be one dollar away from one billion strong. That would make street hustle history. He would shatter records and be forever immortalized in American and even international folklore... He was ready... he was Monster.

"You got that?" the White boy in the suit across the table from Monster asked.

"Fuck I do, come here empty handed?" Monster retorted as he placed the large duff le bag on the table and pulled out a brick of the finest white girl anyone in Pennsylvania had to offer… anyone on the whole east coast, for that matter-of-fact.

Satisfied with the product, the White boy, who had just recently gotten Monster to pitch to him also pulled out a large duffle bag, handed to him from one of his henchmen who were standing behind him. Geno grabbed the money machine and thought he caught something move out of the corner of his eye.

Something was moving near the backrooms, it looked like. He started to brush it off when he say Day Day was also looking exactly where he was. He had noticed It also, Geno observed, because he could see Day Day slowly placing his hand into his pocket where he kept a compact Glock .45 in his True Religion jeans.

Geno made eye contact with Day Day and winked. Day Day did the same thing with Bone Neck until they finally found Monster's eye and gave him the signal.

Shit, it's already ten muthafuckas in here, Geno thought to himself. More than uncomfortable as it is. And now some nigga is running around in the backroom doing who knows what and why, he pondered silently. But Geno wasn't a fool. He knew what to do. He always had a sere for the streets and whenever he ban to feel nervous, he'd touch his gold and chrome with rose gold trimming, Desert eagle .50 caliber to ease the tension.

The nigga was paid. He could afford shit like custom bangers. Besides, he liked guns a lot. Being second in command, he was treated just like Monster was. Even Monster treated him like an equal. But G knew who the boss was. And he knew at least ten reasons why Monster was THAT NIGGA and not himself. But they'd been friends since the third grade and Monster had always been the leader in Geno`s mind. Geno Leaf would die for Monster. He had certainly killed for him. Lately, he'd been trying to really push Monster into the rap shit so his life didn't end in prison or the grave. All these millions, would be a shame if we couldn't spend them, he thought very often.

"You okay, buddy?" the White boy asked Geno, noticing his thoughtful composure as Monster fed the money machine bails of money

"I'm focused on these bricks and this bread, homeboy," Geno said, "like I'm paid to be." he finished, letting him know that shit ain't sweet. "Oh, and I ain't ya fucking buddy." Geno added curtly.

Fat Cat had to shift his weight as he got a good grasp on his four nickel. Day Day was now watching with full awareness so if shit went south these dumb fucks, which he was sure it would, he would know who was where exactly. Day Day having gotten his reputation from lumping niggas back in the day, was not a gun freak like Geno, but he was one of the nicest with a tool, and his hands. That was what he thought made his so special to the set. He knew he could pop three of the four niggas on his right before they could even touch their strap. Day Day was cold hearted and cool headed, yet hot with a burner. Quick to flame a nigga who was out of pocket.

Day Day once slugged a nigga outside a police station in North Philly for trying to rob him ealier that week. It just so happened that they were at the Rally's across the street from the police HQ when he saw the nigga. Day Day pulled out the drive thru line as the nigga walked inside. Day Day parked and went inside behind him. There was an uniformed officer inside named Dagorfield that no one liked. The streets called him Pistol P.G. because he had a reputation for shooting dope boys and getting off with it.

Day Day yanked out his forty cal and blew the niggas top back, and as Pistol P.G. reached for his side arm, Day Day hit him with the rest of the clip, save one. That, he gave as a gift to the nigga lying on the floor motionless with his melon leaking all over the tiles. He put that one right into his cantaloupe too, leaving a baseball sized hole in the dude's head. Day Day raced to his car and was never caught. He was never even an official suspect. North Philly police are so slow, they didn't even get across the street, a five second walk, for a full three minutes after Day Day had left the parking lot. Nobody who worked at the Rally's told on Day Day even though they'd known him from high school. Mostly due to fear, but also because nobody liked Pistol P.G. anyway.

"You got'a bathroom?" Bone Neck asked. "A nigga gotta piss," he explained, not really having to use it, however, he wanted to check out the rear where the movement had come from. He hadn't seen it himself but after the wink from Day Day and the following of his partner's line of sight, he read the signal properly.

"That way," the White boy pointed.

Damn, thought Bone Neck. He was hoping it would have

been down the hall where someone or something was moving. But he went with the flow and went to the restroom anyhow. He took that time to check his two .44 Rugers and put them in the small of his back. Easy access.

Bone Neck liked being in the number one clique. The shine was his enjoyment. He murdered when necessary and was always stunting when he got the chance. Bone liked to shit on people because he was so paid and they weren't Mike Mooney, his government handle, was greedy. And that trait plus his stubborn nature earned him his hook as Bone Neck.

He had only met Monster about three years earlier and quickly made his way up the ladder by following rules and being a loyal asset, thus assuring him the number four spot in 7th Street. All he wanted to know was how could he work his way up to number two and eventually numero uno. He didn't like not being the head of shit but he would just lay low until his time came. Besides, his higher ups were cool. Just not as hot as me, he thought.

"Everything straight?" Bone Neck asked as he came back from the bathroom.

"It's cool," said Geno over the constant noise of the money counter. Then Geno caught more movement again. He could see a mirror in the room at the end of the hall. He had a direct view from the table. Since the door was wide open, he could barely make out something in the mirror. Then his fondness for weapons served him well. It was the barrel of an AK47 in the reflection of the mirror. Someone was holding it with their back to the wall, just inside of the door frame facing the mirror.

Stupid, Geno thought. He didn't like being away from South Philly and he didn't like white people. Mostly though, he didn't like set ups. Geno turned and solemnly nodded to Day Day. The signal was passed through all four.

There were ten in here and how many in the rear, he had no idea. So his constructive mind began to work. Across the table, the White boy in the expensive suit sat with another White boy. The second White dude looked like Jim Carrey. He chuckled silently to himself at that thought.

There were four niggas in street gear behind each of the two White Nikes at the table. That's what Geno liked to call. White people. White Nikes. Another chuckle. Strange, I can find humor at a time where men are about to die... ha ha I may need counseling... yeah, or not, he thought with an edge of sarcasm.

So, he decided that by the dimensions of the hallway and the width of the outside walls, the room wasn't too big. Couldn't be more than three in there, he figured. Thirteen to four. Not bad, he reasoned. But Geno knew they could handle themselves. They were seasoned veterans at young ages, plus this wasn't nearly as bad as he knew it could be. The problem was that these two White Nikes had underestimated them by hiring all these regular niggas who didn!.t look like they could pop a balloon at close range while sticking a needle through it.

True though, Geno had known it was a set up from the moment he first walked through the door. All these niggas in jeans and boodles with two White boys who donned suits? They were recruited and hired to ambush and kill.

He could hear the conversation now, "There aren't going to be too many of them. Just show up and we'll give you guns, ammo, money, and a few kilos for your trouble." Why else would they hire "other" niggas instead of their own? They don't want any of their men dead, that's why. As he thought about it, he figured, that's who's probably in the back with the big boy toys... knowing time was sparse, he decided to act...

CHAPTER 2

THE AMBUSH

With Monster still focused on the money machine, Geno scratched his head and then patted the top of it. Simultaneously, Geno, Day Day, and Bone Neck drew their weapons. Geno focused his beautiful .50 caliber on the apparent leader, while Day Day aimed his forty-five at a random target next to Jim Carrey's look-alike. Bone Neck picked two of the 'other niggas" to concentrate his two .44 Rugers on.

No one spoke a word but the look on the would-be ambushers faces told a thousand tales. Just then, Geno reached under his shirt to his double gun holsters where he held a forty caliber in each. He tossed one to Day Day and then yanked out the other and he targeted another of the stick up boys with it.

Monster, still attentive to the money machine's work, was seemingly unaware of what was transpiring until he finally spoke. "So what's good Fat Cat?" Not even looking up, he continued on quietly, "Y'all muhfuckas think y'all slick, huh?" his words barely audible over the money counter's incessant humming. He was a professional. He knew better than to alert the cavalry in the back room with a loud confrontation. Monster always uses his head.

That's why he's the boss, Geno thought.

"What are you talking..." Fat Cat started as Monster cut him off.

"Shut up," he said, menacingly as he cut Fat Cat's conversation short.

"Who that in the back room, nigga? How many niggas is back there?" he asked, still counting and rubberbanding the paper. He finally looked at Eat Cat and added, "Speak real quiet, bitch. Talk tome, not ya fuckin' monkey in the back room. ain't stupid, nigga. You are. Talk."

Fat Cat sputtered silently, "I-I-1 don't know what you're t-talking about, Monster."

"Geno?" Monster called out.

"Man, it's at least one with an AK back there, Monster," Geno informed him. "Now, who do you think I trust, Fat Cat... him or you bitch?"

Meanwhile, Bone Neck and Day Day moved all the other niggas into the hallway in order to block the view with their backs to the hall itself. They weren't dumb enough to get too close and pat them down because there were eight of them and there were only five guns pointed in their direction.

"Okay, okay. There're only two back there, but I swear they are only here for..." Fat Cat started until Monster cut him off again.

"Bitch, I just said I ain't stupid. Give 'em the signal."

"What?" Fat. Cat said curiously.

"Man, in a minute, I'mma tell Geno to freeze your bitch ass.

You think a nigga playin' with yo' ass, don't you?" Monster spat venomously.

"Okay. Right now?" Fat Cat asked dumbly. Monster remained silent and went back to the money machine, as cocksure as always. That was his answer. "Oh, okay then, thanks. That's good business!" Fat Cat exclaimed loud enough to reach the ears in the back room awaiting this very signal.

Day Day and Bone Neck had moved from in front of the eight niggas because they were aware of how .223 shells could tear through almost anything, especially people.

In what seemed an eternity of silence, Monster and his niggas waited for their ambushers to face them. There is nothing like the advantage of having gotten the drop on a nigga before he could get the drop on you. But even with this decided advantage, a nigga never really knew what to expect, and a gangsta knew to never expect anything. this split second that seemed so forever-like was broken up with a hail of gunfire as the sounds of fully automatic assault weapons rang out. Two niggas had come from the back blazing with reckless abandon. All but one of the eight street niggas placed strategically in front of that very hallway were hit and killed after being ripped apart by the powerful AK rounds. Still, Monster and Geno focused on Fat Cat and "Jim Garrey." Day Day and Bone Neck erased the two gunmen and the lone survivor from the hallway massacre with accurate head shots. Monster constantly had the clique in firing ranges. A trend that had plenty saved his and his comrades lives over the years.

With gun smoke cascading the air and ten dead bodies on the floor, Fat Cat began to cry. "Aww, bitch, shut the fuck up. You started this shit in the first place!" Geno roared.

Right then, two other doors opened in the hallway and two niggas ran out of each room. And them niggas came out hot. Bullets and muzzle flare filled the condo as the deafening roar of the finely crafted Russian assault rifles eliminated the shock of the moment.

This unexpected turn caused Bone Neck, Geno, Day Day and Monster to scatter and regroup their bearings. Monster yanked out a semi-automatic .357 from his belt and took cover just as the other three had. The first two went down quickly as Geno caught one of, them with two to the chest and Day Day hit the other with one in the stomach and another in his neck.

The blood was splattering the walls and ceiling and made the room look like a Picasso of blood.

'BOOM! BOOM!' Bone Neck's .44s rang out loudly and took the life of a third gunman. Three down, two to go, he thought to himself.

The last of the Mohicans began to spray his chopper aimlessly through the apartment with hysteria and fear guiding his resolve. Soon, the chopper stopped as his body hit the floor with a loud thump and a 'CRACK' from his head. Geno caught him in the back of his thinker and damn near took his head off his shoulders with the powerful .50 caliber canon he held.

Jim Carrey's twin had been hit and killed in the melee of bullets and lay still on the floor with body fluids pooling around him. Fat Cat was under the table shaking harder than morraccas. Monster stood up and yanked him to his feet after approaching his hiding spot.

At least we in the middle of nowhere, he thought. Cops woulda been here if we-were in the city and if muhfuckas lived too close. Still though, we gotta bounce, he concluded.

"P.-please, M-Monster! Please don't, man! It wasn't even like that!" Fat Cat cried, pleading for his life.

"Weak ass fag!" Monster screamed ferociously. "Bitch, you tried to fuck us up!"

'BOOM! BOOM! Monster shot Fat Cat in each knee as he screamed out in agony. Fat Cat would never walk again. 'BOOM! BOOM!' Monster shot Fat Cat twice in the head. Fat Cat would never live again.

CHAPTER 3

THE LIFE

"You think we used enough gas to torch Fat Cat's whole spot before the fire trucks and shit get there?" Geno asked as he and Monster approached the Cobb Creek Road exit ramp in Philly.

"Yeah, young bull," Monster said as he surveyed the rearview mirror in order to make certain that Bone Neck and Day Day were still behind them. "We gotta put this work up first, then we gon' have to take these rentals back," Monster said.

"Alright, Monster, but what we gon do with the loot? Shit, we came up with this lil' bit of change. How much was it, anyway? Geno asked.

Monster knew what Geno was thinking. "I was bringin' that nigga the fish: scale, so I hit 'em for fifteen a brick. With the forty bricks, that's six hundred bands," Monster replied.

Geno questioned deeper, "Word, he checks out?"

Monster began to smile. He knew where this was going. He

knew everyone was stacking hard to get millions and to keep them. So niggas rarely got to splurge. Well, he understood that they were already balling harder than anyone else, but they wanted to be reckless with the funds once in a while without setting themselves too far back.

Monster, already being well off, had saved somewhere near ten million. So he figured Geno had to have close to six or seven, easy. But Geno didn't even have two million yet, and Day Day splurged so much that he was pretty much in the same boat. Plus, Monster had to pay so many of his young niggas, police, and various other "law enforcement" officials. He also had mad cribs in and out of the country. He figured he already banked about two million off of the two cds that he had dropped, and by right he should retire from the dope game. But Monster, if you knew him, had always been a man of his word and he wanted to keep his pact, no matter how unrealistic his dream seemed. He made all this paper in ten years and he could only imagine how much more he would earn in twenty.

"Alright, nigga," Monster said knowingly, "we gon' kick it hard. Stupid hard, but. Pull up through McKean Street so we can drop my young niggas on the block some chips. Then lima let Bone Neck and Day Day split the rest. I got me and you, nigga. We can't spend too hard, though. You know Snoop looking for a way to book our cool ass, anyway," Monster finished.

"Man, fuck Snoop! I should bust that crooked ass bitch!" Geno exclaimed.

"Nobody busting no cops, nigga. Remember all that heat when Day Day burnt Pistol P.G. with seven inside Rallys? I had to come out almost three millie to keep that nigga from gettin' knocked," Monster said meaningfully.

"Yeah, I know, Monster. That nigga just be buggin' my nerves, though," G said, defeated.

As Monster thought about it, nobody liked Detective Snoop. Well, except for the other cops and the mayor of course. He had been trying to bank 7th Street for years, and he hated Monster for his slyness and elusive ways. Monster could never be directly tied to any of the crimes that Snoop was sure he'd committed or had a hand in. Plus, all of Monster's young niggas who got knocked always-always-made bail and had the best lawyers. Monster took care of his youngsters so they would never snitch. He had rules to keep them from getting caught with too much work, too many times. If a nigga got time, which was rare, they didn't do long stretches and they had plenty dough on their books. Plus, Monster set them up with a phone to call and they had money and a life to come home to.

Monster ruled his clique with honor and respect. Therefore, his people had mad love for him. It was not fear that held his position, but the greatness that his clique felt with him as the HNIC. Monster was too smart for Snoop and the detective knew it and hated it. Passionately.

"What's good, T.Y.?" Monster asked through the open window to his young block leader as he pulled up on 7th McKean Street.

"Maintaining, Monster. What you know good?" T.Y. said, greeting his boss.

"Shit, shootin' my one-two, young bull. How y'all holdin' up out here?" Monster questioned.

"Ahh, we cool but them 5th Street niggas been wildin' out the last couple of days y'all been gone, nigga," said the young

T.Y.

T.Y. was primed and ready for a higher spot and Monster was ready and willing to give it to him. And he would, in a little while. He didn't really know what spot would be good for the young nigga, so he decided to just think it over until it finally came to him.

One test, then T.Y. would hit pay dirt and he ain't even know it yet. Monster could vouch for his loyalty and character. The young bull had heart but Monster had never seen the young bull kill. He had to be able to stomach that if he was going to move up. But Monster had a good feeling about T.Y. Well, that and the fact that he had heard a story or two about him.

"Fuck them lames, nigga, you got some bread?" Monster asked, knowing he was about to surprise him regardless of his answer to the question.

"You know you keep us trimmed, Monster, but a nigga always on the hunt for more, ya dig? That's why I fucks with you, right?" T.Y. responded with polish.

"Yeah, young bull, sho' ya' right. Look, y'all niggas over here go link up with Toby: and them. Take the night off and come to Club Onix. We gon' wild out, bull!" Monster told T.Y.

"Shi-i-it, you ain't gotta tell me but once, nigga. I'm bout to roll out now and start gettin' fresh fam!"

"Alright, T.Y. but before I forget, here... you know how to divide that Shit up between y'all. you get top, them younger niggas get bottoms. You know nigga's positions, be fair."

"Oh, no doubt, boss man, you know me. I keep it a hunnid everyday, Monster. Damn, how much you got in here?!"

"Not much, 'bout a smooth hundred."

"A hundred what?! Thousand? Aww shit, Monster, you my

muhfuckin' nigga! Damn, this nigga put a whole honeybun in here for us, y'all! That mean I'mma see what... like fifty of this?"

"Don't spend it all in one place, ok? Peace, T.Y."

"Good lookin' out, bossman... peace, Monster."

As they pulled off, Geno started, "Shit, Monster, what's up with them Fifth Street niggas? I don't think that young nigga, Wyan Wyan, feeling us too much. Freeze the nigga?"

"Naw, hold up, G. The nigga only 'bout eighteen. He ain't no threat. Them niggas can't shoot the breeze."

Geno rebuttled, "That's what niggas said about us when we was sixteen and started our takeover, Monster. That's when they started callin° you Monster, nigga!"

"Yeah, I know," Monster said before continuing. "But we was way smarter than them niggas is. They think they some stone cold killas," Monster said passing Geno some kush and a shell. "They think this a fuckin' movie or something. 'If they get outta line then we air 'em out."

"Don't get soft, Monster, we used to ice niggas for less," Geno said.

"Yeah, but damn, nigga, we done murked sixteen niggas today. We only killed more than that in one day when we had Monster Week back in 2013. How many more gotta go this week?"

Geno began to remember Monster Week at Monster's mentioning of it. It was in 2013, when they were just eighteen. The 24th Street niggas was gone get it for robbing every head in 7th Street's top core and then making noise about it in the streets. The 24th Street niggas was deep and they were much older. So nobody thought the young 7th Street niggas were really ready.

Day Day, Geno, Monster, and a couple of other niggas, who were still around in those days, banged twenty-seven niggas in the first 24 hours and seventeen more the rest of the week. On the last day, they went to kick in Duba's door, 24th Street's leader, and emptied four .44s in him. Some called it Monster Week. Others called it Monster Ball. It created the most fear of any clique that had ever touched the pavement in this day and age.

"Alright, Geno, let's go put these whips back and kick it." Monster said. It was time to get back to the life.

CHAPTER 4

LIVIN' LIFE

As Big Sean poured out the speakers in Monster's nightclub, Onix, Day Day, Geno, Monster, and Bone Neck were sitting in their personal V.I.P. area getting sauced. The rain of laser lighting ignited them in a bath of color, highlighting their style and aura. All the meanwhile, the young niggas were on the floor throwing bows and dancing with the broads.

There were about twenty chicks around the V.I.P. section trying to get in and be groupies, and the niggas loved the attention the girls were giving them. As Monster's newest single began to spin, the whole club came to life. Ass was everywhere, weed smoke was floating, and diamonds were shining hard. It was a sea of livelihood and in here, the hood was looking as lively as the sea.

"Now we livin' life!" Bone Neck said with three women hanging on to him. "Get errybody in this muhfucka a drink!" he exclaimed. Then even louder, "Matter of fact, make it two drinks!" He was doing what he loved. Stunting. Day Day and Bone Neck were on the floor now, throwing money and dancing. "Make it rain, bitch! I make it rain on them hoes! Rain Man!" Bone Neck shouted as he made it rain big blue faces.

"How much they end up with, Monster?" Geno asked laughing.

"Nothing by the end of the night. Geno. But they got two hundred a piece."

"Oh yeah, that's bout to be gone!"

It was Saturday. The hottest night to hit Onix in South Philly. Everybody was dressed to impress, others dressed to suggest. Just about every clique was there tonight. 5th Street was there and so were the Money Go Niggas (MGN). 6th Street Killas. Them niggas was death for hire. They murked people for you if you was scared to do the job yourself. They knew who not to fuck with though. The Passyunk Boys was chilling and so were the 28th Street boys. Them 28th Street niggas just club everyday. They all fun and games, just part time niggas for real.

This bad little thing walked past the V.I.P. area and didn't even glance over at the section where Geno and Monster were sitting, sipping Remy and smoking that original purple kush. This type of shit always caught Monster's attention. He didn't like when girls didn't acknowledge him and his presence. Rather, he did like it, for the sense of the chase and the challenge that it produced. Especially with me being THAT ONE NIGGA, all the bitches supposed to want to holla at me, he thought. Even if she's as bad as this one is! he concluded.

About five foot four, caramel complected and her ass in them tight, low cut Chanel capris was tremendous. All this was set off by her C-cup breasts that were nearly D-cups and were full as well as perky. Lips like Megan Good with a walk that might crack the ground, and hair to the middle of her back completed the package. The wearing of much diamonds and being dressed so classily seductive added to the blood flow in his already growing monster.

"Ay yo, who that?" Monster questioned Geno.

"Damn, bruh, I don't know but that little chicken head look like she got some bread," Geno teased. This, coupled with the liquor and weed made Monster really want to have her.

He got up to holler at her before she was lost in the crowd. Monster approached just as the DJ slowed the party down with an old school track. "Come and Talk to Me" by Tevin Campbell was blaring from the subs. Right on time, Monster thought of himself.

"Pardon me, love, may I have a word with you, please," Monster spoke with all the confidence in the world.

"Ummm... I think you just had about ten words with me," she replied with, if possible, even more confidence than Monster himself garnered. He wasn't ready for that witty comeback and she dazed him with the blow.

He bounced back off the ropes, though, as he usually does. "Well, I have to say, I have never enjoyed the speaking of any ten words more than I have those..." he had regrouped quickly and was sure that this counter punch would send her reeling and wanting to throw in the towel. Well, her panties anyway. "So, does that mean that my time is up?" She smiled as he wooed her and he took the smile as an invitation. "Oh, so you know how to smile, too, huh?" He was building momentum now. "So, look, love, I'm not attempting to take up a lot of your time or anything, but I'm wondering if we can leave here and grab something to eat?" No girl can resist free food... even if they'd already eaten, he thought to himself.

"So, you are trying to take up a lot of my time, then? What else you trying to take, boy?" she flirted. Sparring. It was like a sparring match to Monster.

He decided to thow a knock out punch. "I'll take anything you wanna give me, love. And anything you don't wanna give... might as well hand that over too," Monster said smiling. He liked this game. Suddenly, though, her mood changed.

"Sorry, not interested," she frowned. "I'm busy," she said rudely as she stalked away with his pride dragging from her shoe like toilet paper and leaving him looking dumb with confusion.

Fight over... low blow, he thought condescendingly.

"Brat-to-ta-tow!" Geno exclaimed, panomiming an assault rifle aimed at his homie as Monster sat back down. "You got shot down, nigga!" Apparently Geno thought the shit was funny, but Monster didn't.

"I don't understand bitches sometimes, Geno. She went from being on a nigga, to actin' like she ain't know me," Monster surveyed.

"Happens to the best of us, Monster... well, not to me, but it does happen, at least that's what I've been told ha ha!" Even Monster had to laugh at that one. What he didn't know was that she didn't know who he was. She wasn't from Philly and her boyfriend kept her on a short leash, tucked away in the rear all of the time.

"Fay, what the fuck you was doin' talkin' to that nigga?!" Wyan Wyan had demanded of his woman. "That's da fuck why I don't take your dumb ass nowhere. Fuckin' chicken head!"

"Oh, nigga please! I ain't have nothing to say to that funny looking ass nigga. He ain't nobody and you seen I brushed him off, if you was staring as hard as it looked like you was!" Fay shot back.

"Yeah, whatever the fuck ever, Fay. I seen your rat ass, all tee-heeing and smiling, trick. You ain't foolin' nobody. Sit your ass down!" Wyan Wyan fired at her.

"Whatever, Wyan, I ain't worried about that broke ass looking nigga," Fay said lying through her teeth. The nigga was fine and all that platinum and ice set him off, she pondered quietly to her self.

She wanted to leave with the nigga and say fuck Wyan Wyan. He didn't treat her how he did when he first met her in Florida. He brought her to Philly after dating long distance and only seeing him maybe once every two weeks. She knew the nigga was a dope boy but she didn't know he had the type of money that he does. Shit, she thought, I would have been stupid not to come here after he said he was going to get me a condo and pay all my bills.

Even though he was only eighteen and she was twenty-four, Fay knew a gold mine and she didn't mind the age difference except when he acted like he was 15. Just like tonight.

Eventually, she felt like she loved him but his attitude had changed all of that. Now she was just putting up with him until she finished school and could make it on her own. She had decided not to use anyone else for financial gain ever again. This money Wyan provided was paying for her unhappiness. But she wasn't just going to throw it away for free. She was pushing a brand new Tahoe and wasn't ready to lose her plush crib. So she dealt with Wyan's bullshit until she would no longer have to. She rarely even had sex with him because he didn't know how to satisfy her. Then or now. She wasn't cheating on him, though. She was too afraid for that. Now she found herself thinking about the stranger on the dance floor with all of the girls around him.

Fay scolded herself for feeling a bit jealous. The way he moved, she knew that he could satisfy her needs. He. "What is his name?" she asked herself very quietly. Now she wanted to know more than she had first realized. All them diamonds look crazy real, she thought to herself. then she began to wonder if he could possibly have more money than Wyan. Not that it mattered. But I am a pretty girl and I do have needs, she thought solemnly.

"Who da fuck is you staring at, trick?" Wyan Wyan screamed, breaking her fantasy and concentration. "I swear to God, Fay, I should have left your dumb hoe ass in Florida under that fuckin' rock I found you livin' in. Damn bitches don't appreciate a real nigga for shit," Wyan said angrily.

"Ohh, appreciate? That's a four syllable word. Didn't know you knew about those. Learn that all by yourself?" Fay snapped sarcastically.

"Ahhh ha ha! Hell naw, shitted on you!" Herbie Luv Bug said to his number one nigga.

Herbie was Wyan's best friend. He and Wyan Wyan were the top two in 5th Street. They were both trigger happy and extremely wild. "Shoot first, ask questions never" was their motto. Eighteen years old, caked up, and stupid as well, were as close as you could get to describing them. They made money, true, but it was pennies compared to the likes of 7th Street.

Wyan Wyan and Herbie Luv Bug couldn't stand them niggas but they held their peace to a certain degree. No way should they be trying to go to war with such a large giant. In every case but one, David loses to Goliath, and Wyan didn't want to try his luck. But they were growing in numbers and it wouldn't be long until they could try a war with 7th Street, Wyan figured.

I'm sick of making chump change, Wyan Wyan thought, I can't break a quarter millie and these niggas raping the game for millions every single month.

Wyan and Herbie didn't understand how Monster had locked shit down, but then again, Monster and his top three all had some type of education in business management and accounting. Yet, no one from 5th Street even finished high school, let alone had gotten a degree. Plus, no one from 5th Street was even over the age of 21. Add that to the fact that their General, Wyan Wyan, and their Colonel, Herbie Luv Bug, only knew dope and pistols. Point. Shot. Push heroin. That was about the extent of their intellect. But stupidity armed with a weapon is like a nuclear warhead in a crowded mall. Disaster waiting to happen.

"Fuck you, Fay. Stay your ass here, I'm bout to go dance," Wyan said.

"Bye," Fay quipped in response.

As Geno and Monster got back to their seats, Monster caught Fay's eye from the other side of the club, in the other V.I.P. section. Just as Monster saw her, she looked away and he sat down.

T.Y. came and slid next to Monster on the bench style seat of the V.I.P. booth. "Sup, Monster?"

"Shit, cooling out. What's poppin' with you?"

"Bout to bounce with some action in a minute, Yo, I copped a hot whip with some of them chips you put in my pocket today," T.Y. said smiling.

"Damn, bull, already?!"

"Shiiit, nigga, I wasn't wasting no time. Copped a used Lex for twenty-five stacks! Iima boot it up and put some sounds in the trunk tomorrow. While I'm on the block, it's gon' be in the shopping gettin' some screens, sounds, and feet put on her," T.Y. said enthusiastically.

"That's what's up! I'm trying to bounce with this one little chicken head-that I saw earlier. But she acting funny, though," Monster said to T.Y.

"Who?" T.Y. asked

Monster waved at Fay and when she waved back, he got up to go holla at her but she gave him a look that stopped him cold. T.Y. passed Monster the blunt that he was smoking and said, "Ay yo, that's muhfuckin' uh... what's his names bitch. Uh, Wyan Wyan! Yeah, that's his broad. She ain't even from Philly, Monster. She from Florida' The nigga Wyan Wyan tricking tough on her, though. He got her a whip and a crib. Word is she don't even be giving homeboy the pussy all like that!"

"Word? How you be knowing that kinda shit, T.Y.?" Monster asked curiously. "Shit, you hired me to work the streets right? Nobody work the streets harder than young T.Y. And you know the streets be talking, Monster."

I gotta promote this nigga asap, thought Monster. "Yeah,.you're right," Monster said, "I gotta get that bitch though, young bull."

T.Y. responded simply, "I feel that. Do you then. Fuck that hoe ass nigga. Shit, I'm bout to go dance some more. Holla back, young bull. Peace."

"Peace," Monster said in return. It was a good night, Monster was thinking until that bit of information.

"So, I guess we gon' have to freeze) the nigga, huh?" Geno said in speculation.

"Huh? What you mean?" Monster asked genuinely confused.

"Cuz, I know you, "fool and you ain't gon° leave the bitch alone. So that nigga gonna want some wreck. You know he like to shoot shit. he making the streets hot anyway. Let me burn that nigga, Monster. I'll turn dude into a french fry!" Geno said emphatically.

"I know, Geno, but dude ain't did shit to get murked yet. So, chill for now," he said, reaching a staying hand. Silent command to his subordinate. It spoke volumes. "Chill," it said. "It's an order," it whispered.

"Drama" by Meek Mills came on and once again, the whole club gathered and crowded on the dance floor to bang, push, and throw bows. Too much liquor had already been consumed. But the next turn of events was not sparked by alcohol.

CHAPTER 5

SPILLED BLOOD, BAD BLOOD

Shit was moving in slow motion as Monster saw Day Day catch some nigga with a smooth two piece followed by a crushing uppercut, knocking him flat out. Then the brawl began. Security was snatching people up but this looked like... a gang fight. It is! Monster thought, trying to figure out who it was as he rushed toward the action. He had noticed some of his young bulls in the melee.

It was 5th Street. Monster saw that it was Herbie Luv Bug that Day Day had put hands On and dropped to the floor. Bone Neck was stomping the lights out of some other cat and Geno went in swinging, balls to the wall. Monster caught what felt like a haymaker as he went in the crowd. It dazed him, but he had his bearings back quickly.

"What the fuck?!" Monster said, turning toward his assailant and finding Wyan Wyan with his hands up. Fay looked confused as she noticed that the nigga she was talking to earlier was about to fight Wyan.

This is going to be a problem, she thought. Wyan can fight. And that other nigga too pretty to be trying to get dirty with a nigga like Wyan. She had witness Wyan beat the shit out of two people at the same time as they tried to jump him. the next day, the same two were found dead behind an abandoned house.

"What's good, nigga? Let's get it!" Wyan Wyan exclaimed, ready to put hands to his nemesis.

"Damn, bull, now pops gotta punish you," Monster said sarcastically as he tucked in his chain and shuffled his feet.like a pro. "I'mma fucking monster, kid. Time after time, I done told niggas, but niggas ain't trying to listen!" Monster yelled tauntingly. Monster stepped in and feinted the jab. When Wyan Wyan reacted, Monster shot a lightning rod straight right hand that blackened Wyan 's eye almost immediately.

"Oohh wee, I'm out here looking like Mayweather on this boy!" Monster spat as he sent his next three punches with commentary. "Uh oh, left... left, left, RIGHT! Dowwwn goes Frazier!" Monster screamed as Wyan hit the deck after the punishment that Monster dealt him.

Wyan Wyan refused to quit as he showed his resolve by leaping back to his feet. Monster toyed with him. "Damn, kid, that was a five piece chicken nugget, you want some more?"

Wyan whipped a right across Monster's jaw and then followed with a left hook that stung his face. "Ohh, spicy!" Monster teased as he licked his fingers. "I eat that shit!"

Angry, Wyan threw a wild overhand and Monster side stepped it easily, countering with an uppercut to his chin which dazed him. Monster then fed his ribs two vicious left hooks and a murderous right to the kidney. The kidney shot dropped Wyan instantly into the fetal position. "That'll have a nigga pissing blood for a week!" Monster yelled over Wyan's fallen body.

'CLACK CLACK' The sound of a gun cocking caught Monster's attention since the music had long since been cut and the crowd seemed in utter silence as Monster exhibited his superior hand work. It was Geno. Only he, Monster, Bone Neck, and Day Day were allowed to bring pistols inside the club's doors. And right now Geno was fully exercising that right, and brandishing his.

"Fuck up outta here," he said as Wyan got shakily to his feet. He couldn't walk upright and his nose and lip were leaking like project faucets. "Get them niggas up outta here before I do something against my better judgement!" Geno said as the big ass bouncers snatched them up and escorted them out with choke holds and Full Nelsons.

The music was soon resurrected and so was the club's original vibe. This is the hood. Shit happens but the show must go on.

As Day Day, Monster, Geno, and Bone Neck sat in the V.I.P., they exchanged their fight stories, laughing and reenacting them with much emphasis on Wyan getting the shit kicked out of him. The night ended without so much as a hitch after the fight. That's how it usually is... show a couple of niggas a karate movie and they all wanna fight. But show them niggas somebody really getting their ass whooped and niggas is going to cool all the way out.

Everybody went to their own whips to get home and do whatever they were going to do. Bone Neck left with a chick. Geno left with one. Day Day got out with two and Monster decided to play the dolo this night. He was tired and irritated as well. As he exhaled smoke from the cigarello, he slowed the pace of his Wraith. He had just spotted the girl from the club walking home. Alone.

"It's three thirty in the a.m. girl, what you doing walking home by yourself? Somebody might get you," he said through the opening passenger window. He was coasting slowly along the curb to keep up with her and. she still hadn't even looked to find out who her company was. He guessed that she had dealt with more than one stranger pulling up next to her as she walked the streets of Philly.

"Yeah, somebody like you," she fired back, still not looking his way but strolling on.

"True, but you wouldn't let me do ,that earlier " so now I'm stalking you,"

Monster said, toying with her. She finally turned and smiled at his wit and at the recognition of his face as her eyes met his.

As slomnly as possible, she admired his black matte Rolls Royce that was creeping along beside her, rims gleaming in the night air. The smoke black window tinting was impossible to see through but the luxury of the car was impossible to miss. "Hey, boy. Stalking me, huh? Should I call the police?" she teased with a giggle.

"Only if it's an emergency. But for real, love, come get a ride."

As she got in, he asked why she was walking but could afford all of them pricy diamonds that she was flossing. "My boyfriend got mad and left me," she replied, not mentioning that he was the nigga who had gotten his ass whipped by him on the dance floor. She had teased him about it because he always tried to beat on her but got spanked so badly by just one nigga. She smiled at the recollection of the thought, shit it was about time he got trashed.

"Yeah, love, you gotta watch that nigga, Wyan Wyan," Monster said triumphantly. He felt like he knew a secret and had finally gotten to tell it. Besides.; he liked being one step ahead of everybody and everything. Good looking out, Young T.Y!

"How you know?" she asked, stunned.

"This my city, girl. I know more than you think, Ms. Florida," Monster said with a smile before finishing. "You must not know who I am."

She looked exasperated and interested as Monster passed her the weed. He loved when a chick smoked chronic with him.

"Damn! What you do, put an APB out on me, boy?" she asked playfully.

"Well, you're wanted," Monster said.

"By who?" Fay asked seriously thinking this nigga might be some kind of undercover who'd been watching Wyan Wyan.

"By me," Monster replied and threw on his brakes, stopping short in the middle of the empty road and leaned over tokiss her. Fay was a hoe by no means. She never gave the pussy up easy and she definitely didn't kiss people. It had sickened her from the very first time that she'd tried it. However, as Monster thrust his tongue into her mouth, she accepted it and returned hers passionately.

There was something about this stranger that invaded her space. Maybe it was the weed or lack of love that made he take the kiss but whatever it was, she was happy that she did. Fay pushed him away, not really wanting to, but feeling it was necessary.

"That was a nice move. First time that ever happened." Fay

said stunned. I'm really impressed, she thought to herself.

"Impressed?" Monster asked.

Impossible, thought Fay astounded. "Nope." she responded curtly.

"She looked even more beautiful close up. Her facial appeal was literally astonishing. In the dim light he could see her eyes were grey, and lips were full, soft and sweet. She had a perfect smile and the cutest little voice. She sported freckles on the bridge of her nose across the spare of her cheeks. She may have gotten flak for them when she was in elementary school, kids are cruel, but now they only served to highlight her beauty. Every little dot seemed like a dot on a map that lead directly to the most wonderful treasure any man could find.

Monster couldn't remember the last time he could remember so much about a woman. "What's your name, love?"

"Oh, you know my family history, social security number, address and my birthday, but you don't know my name?" she quipped with the hint of laughter.

"Yeah, I hear you. But you gotta leave something to the imagination, right?"

"Fay." she replied.

"Fay what, sweetheart?" I'm sure you were born with a last name, unless they ain't got those in Florida?" Monster said, with a smirk brewing on his face.

"Anyways, boy." she said and she came to the conclusion that she couldn't remember the last time someone asked for her last name before asking for her panties. She liked him already. After sharing her name with him, she asked for his in return. She knew this was someone she definitely wanted to know more about.

"The streets call me Monster. Don't nobody but a few people know my whole name, but go against my rules and tell you. It's Earl, Earl Moore."

"You're Monster?" Fay asked half excited, half uneasy. "Wyan talked about you all the time. The streets been talking too. If you're Monster, then that means you're damn near as famous as a rapper. You do have a nice car and jewels and all that, but nice try, boy. I don't believe you. I ain't no groupie who sleeps with rappers or niggas who claim to be one. "So, fuck you." she said angrily.

Just as Monster was about to respond, he heard the "BLURP" of a police car and saw the beacons flashin in his rearview mirror. He really hated getting pulled over, but he decided to comply anyway. This couldn't be a cop he had

on the payroll.

The officer approaching the window wore plain clothes and swayed toward his beautiful Roils Royce with a confident and knowing swagger. Monster recognized him right off the jump. He sighed dispassionately, knowing exactly what was going on. Monster lowered the winder in anticipation of the coming confrontation.

"What's going on, Monster?" How are you , buddy?" asked a very smug Detective Johnson. His brow hung low, just over his eyes and there were creases at the corners of his mouth. Too much frowning. Johnson's eyes were cast in a deep shade of brown, resembling black, so much so he appeared to be some sort of evil spirit. His attitude matched. Better than average height, his too large head and too long limbs gave him the appearance of one of those Nat-geo images of the caveman. He looked to be a perfect impression of the Neanderthal. "You have the wrong man, Detective. I don't know any "Monster"". My name is Earl Moore, sir." Monster said, putting on his best "white guy" voice.

"Don't give me that bullshit, Moore! I know your alias, I', going to get your sly, mass murdering, dope selling, rapper boy ass!"

"Excuse me, sir, but there's a lady present. If I have, in any way, offended the city's traffic ordinances, I'll properly remove my license, registration, and insurance information so that I may cooperatively assist you in preparing a citation for the violation. That, in which I'll glady pay for any misconduct on my behalf, Detective," Monster replied very condescending and sarcastically. Fay was trying extremely hard not to laugh as the white detective's face became beet red with rising anger and embarrassment.

"Miss, I'd advise someone so pretty not to hang around with scum," Snoop said.

"See, even he thinks you're pretty, love. Not just us scum," Monster said maintaining his condescending tone.

"Fuck you, Monster. Watch your ass!" Snoop said as he began to storm back to his unmarked detectives Dodge Charger.

Before pulling off, Monster decided to fire one last punch in this sparring match... a punch after the bell. "Oh, and he, Detective Johnson? If there was any reason that you couldn't remember what exactly happened here today, if we ended up in court about it, sir... I wouldn't mind bringing in my recording device that is implanted in my Rolls Royce's dashboard. I've made sure to record this very conversation, sir. In case we needed a refresher later on, you know? Thanks, now. Bye bye then... ha ha!" Monster the Asshole, Monster silently scolded himself. He pulled away from the curb, leaving Snoop standing by his cruiser fuming.

"Boy, you is crazy!" Fay said admiringly. She had never heard a street nigga speak so eloquently. She adored a man with intellect. "Sorry for what I said about you earlier," Fay said apologetically.

"It's cool, baby girl. Where am I taking you, to the crib that Wyan Wyan got for you?"

"Damn, there you go peeking in my window again."

"Whatever. Close the curtains."

"Maybe I don't want to."

CHAPTER 6

ALL THINGS NEW

As Monster pulled into Fay's driveway in Upper Darby, he spoke, "Alright, I'mma holla at you. Take my number."

"Where you live, boy?"

"Near downtown, why?"

"It's almost four thirty in the morning. You do not need to be driving all the way back there. And you look sleepy. Poor baby," Fay brooded over him in a motherly tone.

Monster couldn't help but to laugh. He figured that he looked like shit on a stick from being up all night. Plus there was that long as drive back from Fat Cat's spot that seemed to take forever. Damn, its been a long ass day, he thought. He about felt that he was going to fall asleep on the way to her house anyway, so he decided to stay. Of course he had other reasons for wanting to spend the night. Obvious reasons.

He usually bust down more dimes than your average, but he hadn't seen a chick this bad in a long, long time. She was too tempting to resist but he would play it cool, not wanting to appear too thirsty. No matter how much his nature rose at the thought of fucking Fay, he would be passive, not aggressive. Let her come to you, Monster thought silently.

"You sure, Fay? Wyan might try to kill you," Monster said jokingly, yet half serious.

"Anyway, boy, come on. I'm tired, too," she replied.

"Stop calling me 'boy.' I'm grown," Monster found himself saying, though he kind of liked the way she said it. It was cute.

"I don't use nicknames like 'Monster', so it's either that or Early... Boy," Fay chimed in matter-of-factly.

At least she has some class, he figured. "Call me E, then. Don't use my government handle in public," Monster said.

"I'll think about it," she responded affectionately.

Fay opened the door to her condo and flicked on a light. Monster always kept an overnight bag in all of his whips for times like this, and he brought it in with him. "I need a shower, Fay. Where your bathroom and guestroom at?"

Damn, Fay thought, he asked about the guestroom? He definitely ain't like the rest of them. he ain't even assume that he's getting some ass just because he's spending the night. I hope I can contain myself. It's been a long time, she thought as she remembered how easily Monster moved about the dance floor with such a sensual vibe.

"Bathroom there," she pointed, "Your room there, right next to mine," she hinted.

"Thanks," he responded. Monster dropped his bag in the room and after grabbing what he needed for a shower, went straight to the bathroom with the towel wrapped around him. Meanwhile, Fay was microwaving some left over spaghetti from earlier. She figured they'd need something to put on their stomachs before bed.

Monster had the habit of leaving the shower on after he got out of it. He usually dressed first, then returned to turn the shower off. It was an annoying habit that he'd had since he was a child. He did it unconsciously and this time he had done it again. He wrapped the towel around him after stepping out of the still running shower and went to the guestroom unnoticed.

Fay was thinking to herself that Monster really takes long showers when she remembered something. "Oops, I forgot to put clean sheets on the bed," she said to herself aloud. Herbie Luv Bug and Wyan Wyan had spent the night a couple of days ago. It was funny, as she thought about it. She wouldn't give Wyan the pussy so he went to sleep in the guestroom with Herbie. Like that would make me jealous, she giggled to herself silently. She grabbed some fresh linen and went to make the bed before Monster could get out of the shower. She opened the door and was met by the surprise of a lifetime.

There stood Monster with the light on, attempting to dry himself off. Naked. Fay gasped as the bright overhead light shone upon him with revealing intensity, offering an unobstructed view of his five-foot-five and a half inch frame and 'his immaculate build. His arms and chest bulged from hard, toned muscle and his legs were thick and strong.

She surveyed his abdomen and figured she couldn't buy a better six pack. Knowing she was dead wrong, she couldn't pull her eyes away from him, nor could she find the strength or will to leave the room. Fay was mesmerized by the sight of such an amazingly build man. He had tattoos all over the place and Fay loved body art. She especially loved the work of art that his body was and its most defining member rose to salute her. Long and thick, she thought as she took in the sight of E's monster.

He didn't even attempted to cover himself. He enjoyed the look on Fay's face, who had been standing speechless in the doorway for all of three seconds. He just grinned as her tongue seemed about ready to just drop to the ground. "You didn't knock." Monster said quietly.

"I'm sorry. I didn't know you... umm... uh." Fay said stumbling over her dialogue. She couldn't find her thoughts. Her brain, her tongue, and her heart were all wrapped up, tied in a confusing knot that was centered around her throbbing, pulsing hormones. She was in ring heat as she took in this specimen of a man.

"That's not a knock either, but it'll do," Monster said seductively, throwing his towel to the floor. "Come on in, the water's fine," Monster said temptingly. His blood was running wild as his hormones chased. Fay hesitated and reluctantly stepped forward. She was in a fantasy, and yet the dream was real.

Monster seemed to glide over to her. he found a spot on her neck to place his warm mouth and roaming tongue. Fay moaned and her panties were instantly soaked. "I made us dinner," she said moaning. "We ain't even eat yet," she finished.

"We bout to right now," Monster said. Passion loomed between them and was nearly thick enough to cut with a knife. Monster ripped open Fay's shirt and she gasped with pure eroticism. She began to unbutton her pants and Monster slapped her hands away and placed them behind her back as he was still wandering over her glorious hotspot with his seemingly omnipresent tongue. he unbuttoned her capris after she stepped out of her high priced Louboutin shoes. Once she'd wiggled out of her pants, Monster removed her bra and then snatched off her thongs. Both acts accomplished with just one hand.

His mouth found hers as he cupped her breast with one hand. Monster moved behind her and rested his dick between her mountainous ass cheeks, one hand arousing a nipple, the other teasing her clitoris. He let his mouth roam more passionately over her neck and ear.

Fay shuddered as gasps and moans escaped her uncontrollably and it became more difficult to stand. She had never been in this much ecstasy and they hadn't even fucked yet. She could feel him rock hard, pressing against her ass and she began to grind slowly on his swollen dick. As he picked up the pace on the three spots that he was focusing on, Fay's fluids started to flow increasingly. She was near climax when he plunged his finger suddenly into her opening. He did his work masterfully and upon his finger entering her, she screamed and orgasmned simultaneously.

She buckled at the knees-and Monster held her up as she finished her orgasm. He then lifted her easily and placed her on the bed. Fay had cum for the very first time by a hand that was not her own. She was astonished... they hadn't even had actual sex. Yet.

Fay wanted to return the favor and as soon as Monster got onto the bed, she pushed him on his back and climbed his body with lust highlighting her eyes. She let her tongue explore his neck and chest and it was his turn to moan. He shook, trembling under the expertise of Fay's tongue as it traveled down into the depths of the long, dark, deep. Taking him completely into her mouth and giving him supreme neck caused him to grab at the sheets and nearly curl his toes until they touched his heels.

As Monster felt ready to bust his nut, he stopped Fay. It wasn't time. He knew, the way that they carried on, that, after one, he would be done because it would be a big one. She had him building up for an explosion. Monster then lay Fay on her back and showed her a tongue twister. He licked her and sucked on her sweet nectar until she once more lost control and orgasmed again. She couldn't believe that she had two orgasms within such a short amount of time. This was something that she hadn't ever experienced before. Her mind wandered as she traveled through space. Monster came back up to her voluptuous breasts and found her pussy with the head of his universal soldier.

"Me... strong like bull," he teased with a fake Native American accent as he entered her and filled every nook and cranny she had. He moved slowly into a strong, quick, passionate, and deep thrust. Constantly changing his rhythm to keep her off balance and off guard.

Monster popped his clutch and worked his stick with better control than a race car driver. Monster had to hit it from the back. It was a mandatory rule with girls who had fat asses. As she turned over, she arched her back and lifted her ass high into the sky and her dripping pussy invited him in with a warm welcome and a firm grip. Almost like a handshake, he thought privately to himself.

Fay threw her ass back at him and Monster caught it as they moved together in glorious union. And he pounded her into exhaustion until the time came. And when the time came, they came together. Shaking, moaning, screaming and finally, sleeping.

CHAPTER 7

°NOTHER DAY, °NOTHER DOLLAR”

"Dem, muthafukcas got me fucked up!" Wyan Wyan yelled to Herbie Luv Bug the next day as Herbie walked through Wyan's front door.

"Man, this shit started cause you can't control your bitch, nigga," Herbie said honestly.

"Fuck we gon' do Wyan? Them niggas is damn near untouchable. Ten years, nigga! They been in the game bout ten fuckin' years, bull," Herbie whined. "Their squad is mad deep and them niggas is loyal. Fuck we gon' do?!" Herbie Luv Bug finished sadly.

"Man, fuck that shit. Everybody can be touched. It's just about how far you gotta reach, fam," Wyan Wyan concluded.

"Aww, bitch nigga, that's about the only smart thing you ever said... ha ha! Herbie Luv Bug jumped in teasing.

"Nigga, fuck you. Anyway, I'mma fuck Fay bitch ass up, too. This shit is her faulth," Wyan said even angrier.

'Naw, nigga. You gotta take some credit for tellin' me to

swing on him. You know I don't refuse no order. Nigga. Yo top gorilla so ima do what you say.

"I agree with everything you saying, right, but the question still remains, what the fuck we gon' do?" Herbie questioned realistically.

"Hold up. I don't even know yet. Let me call Fay to see if she made it home last night in one piece. I shouldn't have left her that way, for real," Wyan Wyan said apologetically.

"I shouldn't have left her last night... ohh, I love her, Herbie... boo hoo! Beat it nigga! You know what, Wyan, I think you on some real live bi-polar shit. Ha ha!" Herbie Luv Bug said after sarcastically mocking Wyan with whining and fake crying.

"Fuck you, Herbie!"

"Hello?" Fay answered sleepily.

"It's fuckin' twelve o'clock in the afternoon, Fay. Fuck is you doing still sleep?!" Wyan Wyan demanded into the receiver.

"What?" Fay asked still not fully able to concentrate on what Wyan was screaming about. It's always something with this nigga, she pondered.

"Can... the... fuck... you... hear... FAY!" he said as if she was slow, deaf or hard of hearing. "Fuck is you doing still asleep? You fucking heard me the first fucking time," Wyan said angrily.

"Damn, Wyan, you sure is cussing a lot lately," Herbie said laughing.

"So, nigga, you sure is stupid a lot lately," Wyan shot back.

"Who?" Fay asked, not aware of who Wyan was talking to. She'd just come out of her groggy haze and remembered that Monster was lying next to her, and smiled. She was thinking of round two already.

"Not you, you fuckin' dummy. Did I fucking say 'Fay`? How the fuck did you get home last night?" Wyan said breaking her train of thought.

'Stop saying 'fuck' so much. Makes you look bad," Herbie said with laughter. He knew the more angry Wyan got, the more he would take it out on Fay. So he would agitate him accordingly. Besides, he personally was sick of the dumb bitch. Plus she ain't giving up no ass anyway, he thought.

"Fuck you, Herbie! And fuck the fuckin' fuck!" Wyan called out as Herbie Luv Bug burst into raucous laughter, causing him to fall over in agony and clench his stomach.

"How you think I got home, nigga," Fay answered rhetorically.

"Nigga? Bitch you don't ever call me 'nigga'. Who over there?" Wyan demanded.

"Wha-what you talking about, boy? You just paranoid."

"Naw, bitch, I ain't dumb. You fucking somebody else, that's why you won't gimmie no pussy, ain't it? I'm on my way, bitch. BYE!" Wyan exclaimed slamming the phone down, nearly breaking his iphone.

After hanging. up, Herbie Luv Bug just smiled. He knew this was going to be good. he had to ask, "Can I come, too?"

"E, get up! Get up! Wyan is on his way over here!" Fay cried out loudly.

"So, let me know when he gets here so I can beat his ass again. And I'm still tripping about how this nigga still ain't getting no pussy from you, ha ha."

"You silly, but for real, you gotta bounce before he gets here. He will shoot you, boy! That nigga be killing people. I hear him and Herbie talking all of the time, E. Why you looking at me like that?"

"I thought you said you heard of me," Monster said. "Why you think they call me Monster, huh? I ain't ugly, girl. I act ugly," Monster said and reached his hand under the mattress and pulled out his semi-automatic .357 and laid it on the nightstand with a powerful 'thud' as the metal met the wood in a sound of death on a march. "I'mma fucking monster. I'm The muhfuckin' Monster," he proclaimed proudly.

Fay gasped and the sight of the huge pistol almost made her fall backward off of the bed but she held her composure. Wyan Wyan never brought guns out around her. This was the first time she'd seen one so big. Without taking her eyes off of the canon, she spoke, "Pleas go. I can't lose my house over this..." she began.

"This what? Damn, shorty, if its like that then, yeah, I'm out. Holla."

Fay didn't want to hurt his feelings and she didn't think there was anymore to this than a fuck. She, of course, thought she wanted more but she wasn't sure that he did. "No, no. It's not like that, E. I don't even know what you want but you don't even know me and I've got bills. he pays them all, so what am I going to do if he kicks me out? Be homeless?" Fay said sincerely. Although she had ridden in his Rolls Royce the night before, Fay was ignorant about cars, like a lot of women were. She could easily see that it was a super luxurious vehicle but that didn't really register in her mind. She only knew what kinds of cars cost a lot of money... she didn't know what kind of car was what until it was pointed out to her.

Monster thought to himself that this was the prettiest face

he'd ever seen, and the most gorgeous body a woman could ask to possess. "Baby girl, I make more money in a week than your boy got saved up. I'mma bounce, but don't forget to call. I wanna know you," Monster said to her confidingly. They got a quickie fuck in and Monster left Fay relaxed, satisfied, and wet. Three things she had not been in a long time.

When Wyan Wyan got there, he beat Fay's ass. She was ready to call Monster and tell him but she didn't She'd just wait until the scars and bruises healed before she saw him again. The scars would heal, but the pain wouldn't. Something would have to change... soon.

CHAPTER 8

CHANGE

SIX MONTHS LATER...

"Where you gon' tell him? Over the phone?" Monster asked Fay into his cell phone.

"Let me hit that, Monster," Geno said to Monster.

"Here, nigga. I'm listening, love. Go ahead."

"No, I'mma have to have him come through and tell him to his face. After all this time, he deserves that, at least."

"That nigga don't deserve shit, if you ask me. Except for an ass whooping. But if that's how you feel then that's how you feel. I'm all the way in West Philly, so ain't no way that I can be there to protect you if something goes wrong, you heard? Tell you what, I'mma send Bone Neck over to the crib to lay low and make sure shit go straight."

"Okay, baby. I love you."

"Yeah I love you, too, baby girl. Holla." As Monster hung up, he turned his attention to T.Y. without taking his eyes off of the road. "T.Y. make that call to Bone Neck for me, my nigga."

"Yo, this Bone Neck. What's up?... Who?... Fay?... When?... Yeah, yeah, aiight. Alright, T.Y. It's on... peace," Bone Neck said ending his conversation with T.Y. bitterly. "Man, this nigga, Monster, still got me on this bullshit!" Bone Neck screamed to one of the young block huggers. "I'm sick of this shit!" he yelled as he got into his whip and sped off aggresively.

"Shit, Monster, that nigga ain't sound too happy. Especially not having to take orders from me. How long he on time out?" T.Y. asked curiously.

"I don't even know. That's what the fuck happen when you disregard orders. Actually, what usually happens is a nigga come up stanking, you feel me?" Monster said beginning to think about that day five and a half months ago when Bone Neck made a deal with some funny bunny ass niggas.

Monster told Bone Neck not to fuck with these lames because some shit was stinking. And when some shit stinks, it's because you're smelling shit. But Bone Neck, being hard headed and greedy, went behind his back to make the deal anyway. All he was thinking about was his own pockets and a higher spot in the clique. "Never happen," Monster said quietly to himself. "Never."

Dude supposedly had two million on hand and he wanted Monster to get him the best shit he had. So Bone Neck took eight young street goons that were just following orders they thought were legit, and went to Delaware on some sneak shit. But lo and behold, the shit was a set up. It was the age old play. The buyer was an informant hoping for a shorter prison stint. Bone Neck got four of his young niggas locked up, two got murked, and the other two made it out with him "in a blaze of glory" so to speak. They ended up killing four feds and the informant, though.

That ship pissed Monster off SD much that he moved Bone Neck back to block leader status. he lost a lot of money, power, and respect being demoted and that shit sat hot on him.

The only reason that Monster hadn't killed the nigga was because he brought back the money and the work. But now he got four young niggas in boiling hot water with the feds, and Monster's busting his ass paying lawyers to get them kids an out date or a technicality to get them free. Both were long shots but money talks and it usually holds long conversations. He kept their books tight hit he couldn't have any contact with them, otherwise he might be implicated.

So everything he did for these kids was through an attorney which hid him entirely. He knew they would never talk. Loyalty. All of his men had that quality. But he was beginning to wonder to whom some of theirs actually belonged to.

"So, what, Fay 'bout to tell Wyan she moved in with you and he getting that boot now?" Day Day asked.

"Yup yup. 'Bout fucking time, too. She acting all scared and shit. I be telling her, I got this, you feel me?" Monater replied.

"Yeah, I feel you. How much further, Monster? Last time we came this way we had to fuck Fat Cat's bitch ass up. We gonna always remember that," Day Day recalled.

"Yeah, we are. That's why I took extra precautions this time. I hope this shit runs smoother than last time," Monster responded hopefully. Hope. The essence of things not seen.

CHAPTER 9

BIG TROUBLE IN WEST PHILLY

Monster and Geno sat in the apartment complex with the money machine working away. De ja vu, Monster thought. Once more, this was his first time doing business with somebody and they happened to be from West Philly.

Two other men were in the apartment with them, happy that they were able to do business so smoothly. They weren't as much happy about the deal as they were about the bust. Law enforcement... they lived for it.

"You got the work?" M.T. asked Monster as he was still counting money.

"Fuck I do, come here empty handed?" De ja vu... "Yeah, I gotta make sure you check out first," Monster shot back. Monster had learned not to trust these West Philly niggas anymore. Especially after that shit with Fat Cat and then that Delaware shit with Bone Neck. So he was glad to take extra precautions this time around.

Monster had decided to give this nigga, M.T. a fake alias along with a few more safety valves. They brought different ammunition this time _lust in case they got banked. They didn't want what they did last time to come back and bite them in the ass because of ballistics. On top of all that, they bought a "scrubbed" car that no one could trace back to them. Day Day and T.Y. sat in the whip outside the complex for long distance cover. Just in case. Chance favors the prepared mind.

Monster was really proud of T.Y. lately. Loyal and cool headed, plus he was smart. Monster liked him so much that he gave T.Y. Bone Neck's spot. No one had ever made it to number four so quickly. Two years of block burning and now he was making his first big move. He'd get about two hundred thousand for this trip and didn't even know it yet. Monster was killing the game. he bought bricks for five per slab and was making almost ten times that sometimes, depending on the purity of the product and where it was going. It was an unspeakable, one-in-a-million deal, he knew. But when you're Monster, you get those kinds of connects. He had merely saved one Colombian's son. The little dude got hit by a car downtown and Monster scooped him up and got him to the hospital in time to save his life. He didn't wait on an ambulance, he didn't call the authorities. He just acted. That was always in him... act. And act quickly. Don't think. Don't hesitate. Act. Because of that, he earned a lifetime deal on everything he wanted.

Day Day and T.Y had serious heat in the scrubbed vehicle. It was a newer model Impala purchased through a proxy buyer for cash. They had then scratched off the VIN numbers and placed passable license plates on it. Inside with the two men were 2 Ak47s, 2 U.S. AS12 fully automatic shotguns, and an asshole load of ammo along with a few pistols.

Monster was taking no shorts this time, that's why he left the real dope in the car and took the fake shit in with him and Geno. Monster and Geno had also used_an Uber from fifteen minutes north of the meeting spot so that they could be dropped off without bringing attention to Day Day and T.Y. When the Uber picked up Monster and Geno, Day Day and T.Y. followed at a distance. They pulled in the parking lot about five minutes after they were dropped off. This plan was to throw off any possible surveillance. Monster was on it. No shorts. No losses. He played it cautious. Just in case.

Monster sat the bag on the table after bagging up the money and M.T. asked again, "So, now you know its all there, where's my work?"

Geno unslung his huge duffle bag and Monster was about to tell M.T. That it was fake once he opened it, but he stopped short of saying anything. What had forced him to pause was the look on M.T.'s face when he opened the duffle. His eyes had nearly bulged from his face when he saw the exposed cream. Monster knew that face meant bad news. M.T. was too excited about something that he should be used to seeing.

"We got it, we got it!" M.T. began shouting.

Monster and Geno reached for their pistols just as about fifteen sheriffs and All officers ran into the apartment after barging into the apartment. "Awww, shit," was all Monster could say.

"What the fuck?!" Day Day exclaimed as he watched about eight unmarked cars pulled into the parking lot and armed personnel rush into the building. T.Y. and Day Day got real low so as not to be seen. Day Day reached into the backseat and grabbed an AK and loaded it with a magazine. He reached up to the slide and bolted a .223 in the barrel. The sound was lethal as the death in a full metal jacket was ratcheted into its ready to kill position. He repeated the same process for each of the other pieces of artillery that they'd brought.

"Fuck you think you doing?" T.Y. asked in disbelief.

"I don't know yet, young T.Y. Just be ready for anything."

"What's your fucking name?" screamed the lead officer on the raid squad.

"Elvis-," said a smirking-Monster. "Elvis Pressley. And his name is Lisa Marie," he joked as he nodded toward the direction of Geno. The agent was hot about Monster's tendency to be an asshole.

"You fucking nigger!" The White Pate officer called Mixson spat with venom.

"Damn, he said it with the 'E-R' at the end. Now there's a racial slur if I ever heard one," Geno said in his best White guy voice. "That was very insulting, sir. But don't worry, thanks for the hospitality anyway," Geno said with a smile, making Monster suppress a laugh.

"You little fucks got one coming. I know you had something to do with that mass murder drug deal six months ago. Now tell me your names before I have to take you in for prints," said Mixson.

Now he was fishing. Knowing they didn't have a record, Geno and Monster remained quiet. They joked, but were fully aware of the trouble the situation would cause. Even though the work was fake, they could still be charged for it, and also be brought up on conspiracy and weapons charges. And they would still be in prison forever and a day. Plus, with the feds, they always get their man. Then the Good Cop, Bad Cop scenario began.

"Sarg," said another of the ATF agents. This one was black. Go figure, perfect for the situation, Monster thought. But I ain't stupid, he concluded silently.

"Take it easy, Sarg. Sorry about that, fellas..." Then the "Good Cop" went into character and gave a long drawn out speech about helping themselves before the shit hit the fan. He talked to them about wanting to see them get out as soon as possible and how he knew they didn't mean any harm. That they knew they were just trying to feed their families and didn't really want to be doing this.

He's good, thought Monster. Not that good though.

Then the Black detective finished with, "Now, look, fellas, tell us your names and you'll leave in my care, under my eye. Or if not, he's going to take you guys."

"A cop's a cop," Geno said.

Then Mixon broke in again, "Fucking tell me your cockerfuck sucking names or I'll personally beat the shit out of you!"

"Umm... I'll take the right to remain silent for five hundred, Alex. And what's a cockerfuck?" Monster said as he and. Geno could no longer contain their laughter. They laughed until they cried and their stomachs hurt. None of the officers like this one bit, so they began beating Monster and Geno with hard body shots and kicks. The fists and feet rained down on their intended targets with brutal precision. It felt like they were being hit with sledgehammers and iron fists filled with buckshot. The handcuffs they were in didn't aid their situation one bit because they could not block nor protect themselves from the officer's brutal onslaught. All they could manage was to curl themselves up into a tight ball and take the punishment that was delivered to their exposed bodies in the fetal position.

"Let's get these fucks outta here before the news cameras get here," Mixson said with sweat dripping from his brow. The cop was huffing and puffing his way to that seemed like a heart attack, but he wore a smile as if to say the beating of drug dealers was his true passion. And judging from the enthusiasm in which he partook in the ass kicking, it just may have been. "I don't care how fake this shit is, I'm nailing you dickheads for these guns and for packaging with intent to sell counterfeit narcotics. I'm sure conspiracy will come along and some other place has got to be looking for you guys," he said smugly. With that, he began to smile suspiciously.

"Ah, shit," Monster said under his breath, "This about to be fucked up."

Wearing gloves, Mixon lifted the nine-millimeter that Monster had been carrying and walked over to M.T., the snitch that had set them up from the get-go. "Here," Mixson said to the confused informant. M.T. outstretched his hand very reluctantly and was knocked off of his feet with two quick shots to his chest.

The crooked cop stood over his lifeless body and dumped another bullet into the already dead informant's head. The blood splatter was tremendous, the impact was astounding, and the retort from the SW was deafening. Everyone who could, covered their ears.

"You know he dead," Geno whispered through his teeth.

"Now you shit trucks have a murder that I'm sure is going to stick," the cop said laughing. For the next ten minutes he and the other cops went over a good story that they would report in their arrest records before they called in the shooting. Turns out that they were a dirty band and Dead M.T., formerly Not Dead M.T., was new to their unit and was threatening to expose them. They had obviously done this before.

"Were fucked," Monster said in a hush.

"Hope not," replied Geno. Hope... the essence of things...

"Alright, boys, let's get 'em outta here," the Black cop said. He and Mixson yanked Geno and Monster up to their feet and readied them for transport. "We're leaving. Brimmer, You're lead 'till we get back to the 'crime scene'."

"Yes, sir," the cocksucker replied enthusiastically.

Fuck, fuck, fuck, thought Monster. This is bad. He knew that his prints would not be on the gun, however. He and the rest of the crew would rub liquid band-aid on their hands when-they knew something that may involve killing or prison was going to happen. When the liquid band-aid dried, it erased fingerprints by smudging them for a few days. But, he thought, they'll eventually get us on an officer's testimony. We're fucked, the long way.

"They been in there for like thirty minutes," T.Y. said from the driver's seat. "I wonder who got popped."

"Look," Day Day said pointing to the door that had just opened with two cops, one White and one Black, leading Monster and Geno out in cuffs. He breathed a sigh of relief and his heart leapt with joy, knowing they hadn't been shot or killed by any of the three rounds that they heard go off—The cops held the duffle bags in their gloved hands. The money and the set-up work, Day Day supposed.

Geno and Monster were placed in the back seat of an unmarked cruiser while the cops sat the bags up front with them. After they pulled off, Day Day spoke to T.Y. "Follow them."

"The fuck we gonna do, Day Day? It's over, baby. We can't do shit!"

"You gotta have faith, Young T.Y. I'mma teach you what ten years taught me. Gotta learn to find an opening. Just follow 'em and when I tell you, pull up on the driver's side, aught?"

"Alright, Day Day, man, don't do no crazy shit."

Day Day grabbed an AK from the back. The vests the cops were wearing would not stop an AK47 round if they were wearing two of them shits, Day Day thought smiling.

"Aww, man. You 'bout to do some crazy shit. I just asked you real nice like. Remember? I said, 'Please don't do no crazy shit, Day Day.' But here we go anyway, T.Y. complained shaking his head in frustration.

"Ha ha, muhfucka, you ain't say "Please?" If you did, I wouldn't have thought about what we gonna do," Day Day laughed out.

"Okay, then. Please?" T.Y. pleaded.

"Ha ha, too late, ill' nigga. Let's get it," Day Day said with a knowing smile.

Monster nudged Geno and looked back out the rear windshield to give him the ups that Day Day and T.Y. were right behind them.

"They can't do shit," Geno whispered.

"You know Day Day," argued Monster, matching Geno's whisper.

"Ray Ray? Ray Ray, who?" asked the nosy White cop. Mixson was up front ear hustling. Poor job of it too. They decided to shut up before they fucked up and got Day Day and T.Y. knocked, too.

"Honk the horn hard," Day Day told T.Y. as the light up ahead turned red. "Then pull up on the side fast and hard. They'll be distracted and confused, not to mention off balance. Stop quick next to their car. GO!"

'H-O-O-O-ON---NNKKK!' The sound that came from behind the unmarked cruiser as they stopped at the traffic signal was a blaring horn. The sudden alarm jostled the passengers immediately and the car's occupants all turned around to

look7± behind them just as T.Y. unexpectantly yanked up on the driver's side. Still searching for a car behind them, someone screamed and startled the driving Black cop and Mixaoui. They both turned to face the sound and so much more.

"HEY!" Day Day yelled into the lowered window of the unmarked cruiser next to them. As soon as they had the cops' attention, the murder in Day Day's eyes became evident and unstoppable. The cop's mouths dropped at the sight of an. AK47 barrel pointed directly at them. The Black cop attempted to speed off but he was too late. The murder was coming. It was coming with the speed of an assault rifle ejecting its death into its intended target. He barely had time to blink.

'BRA-TA-T-TA-TOW!' The Ak47's powerful blasts ripped into the car's front seat, completely devastating and dismantling both officers. The bodies jumped and bucked around inside the cockpit as Day Day emptied the entire thirty-two round magazine. Monster and   ducked low as both blood and bullets spattered the vehicle.

T.Y. threw the car in park, hopped out of the driver's seat quickly, and headed over to the destroyed police cruiser. He grabbed the keys and duffle bags and let Geno and Monster out as Day Day moved into the driver's seat of the getaway car.

T.Y. then shot each cop in the head with his .45 so that there was no chance of a miracle. T.Y. hopped into the passenger seat and tossed the keys to Geno so he and Monster could free each other. They then pulled off after murdering two cops in broad daylight.

Civilian vehicles in the area who noticed the massacre sped away with reckless abandon or fear for their own lives. A few of the citizens stopped their cars, awestruck at the scene. Until Geno let off a few rounds in the general direction of a few of the onlookers. That put a fire under their asses alright. If the initial outburst from the AK hadn't moved them, then those warning shots did.

"Day Day, my muhfuckin' nigga!" Monster screamed. "Y all two niggas get a bonus. A big, funky, fat ass bonus! Fuck, I love y'all. Let's roll bro. Not too fast though, 'cause I don't want to draw attention to us. I know somebody in traffic had to call nine-one-one after seeing all that shit we just pulled. They probably already got a description and a license plate number. Always assume the worst," Monster said, still thinking like a boss.

"Hell yeah, good looking out, y'all! We thought it was over for a minute. Shoulda known Day Day crazy ass was gonna pull some shit out the hat, though," Geno added thankfully.

"Yes, and I specifically asked him not to do some crazy shit," T.Y. laughed indulgently. Just then, a police car came flying out of the intersection ahead of them. After he blazed past them, all four let out a sigh _of relief. Then breathed a breath of contempt as the cop car wheeled around to pick up on their tail.

"Fuck, fuck, fuck, fuck!" Monster exclaimed. "Fuck it! Car

chases? We do those too," Monster roared proudly. "Load the fuck up, y'all. Geno, pass me that damn street sweeper. Let's get nutty!"

After everyone checked his weapon and knew exactly what they had to do, Day Day and T.Y. fretted over changing their positions. Day Day wanted to shoot and no one knew what T.Y. could do in their current situation, and this was a problem. But the police cruiser was fast gaining on them, so a decision would have to be made. Quick.

"Fuck it," Monster yelled again. "T.Y. just do your thong, young bull. You shot an AK before, right?"

"Yeah, -yo-J,, I'm ready. We went to the range a few times on our own and I made sure I got familiar with plenty of guns," T.Y. replied, eager to prove his worth.

T.Y. moved first, pulling his upper torso out of the passenger window as Day Day floored the pedal on the city streets. T.Y.'s assault rifle sprayed the front of the cop car and fiery death hit the driver four times in the chest, splattering the inside of the vehicle with gore in a wash of crimson delight. The car then flipped about five times and two other cruisers appeared, in hot pursuit of the 7th Street getaway.

"I likes this young, nigga!" Geno blared loudly.

Day Day, meanwhile, had the car on skates, surfing in and out of traffic, weaving better than a spider web. Car horns were blaring, colors streamed past like fast moving crayons as their speed approached 50, 55, 60 miles per hour. Day was moving the car like Dale Earnhardt Jr. He was focused on his mission. Getaway. Gone in sixty seconds. Or die.

Since the rear window didn't roll all the way down, Monster used the butt of the large automatic shotgun to knock out the glass and then extended his own upper torso out, as well. Geno lifted himself out of the sun roof, clutching a fully loaded AR-15 sporting a banana clip with 75 rounds, ready for warfare.

The officers were handcuffed, so to speak, unable to fire back any shots in traffic, as protocol would not allow them to shoot from a moving vehicle in the vicinity and presence of pedestrians and civilian vehicles on a crowded city thoroughfare.

Monster's street sweeper began to wreak havoc as he let loose rounds of explosive shells. The powerful automatic spotty blasted the passenger of a cop car as he began to fish tail across the road. The windshield dissipated after being riddled with holes as Monster watched the officer's body splash blood all over the driver and the interior. It was like a gruesome painter slinging red paint in order to complete his master work.

Geno and Monster released the entirety of their clips into the injured vehicle, completely stopping and immobilizing it. They began to hoot and holler with pride when the car went up in flames and the driver came flying out the drivers side, on fire. The human torch was mowed down viciously by an eighteen wheeler who couldn't seem to be able to stop.

While Monster and Geno reloaded, T.Y. sprayed at the remaining car. "Hang on, y'all!" Day Day screamed. He then maned the brake and the emergency lever, and whipped the challenger into a full one hundred and eighty degree turn in the busy street. After the quick professional like maneuver, all guns focused on and literally disintegrated the police car they were now passing.

"Swiss Cheesed that bitch!" T.Y. yelled.

A police car was coming at them head on and was coming

fast. Day Day was thinking to himself that this game of chicken was lose-lose. "T.Y!" Day Day yelled, yanking on his pant leg with his free hand as he steered expertly with the other. "Shoot out the windshield of our car!"

T.Y. sat back inside the car and after blasting out the windshield, he kicked it out. Day Day's and T.Y.'s ears were ringing from the sound of the machine gun's tremendous explosive sound. Raising himself back out the car's window, T.Y. began to fire at the cruiser coming fast toward them head on. His shooting was in vain, as he could not damage the car at such a distance with the Ak47 jerking and bucking with recoil in his grasp.

As if things couldn't get any worse, two more cars came flying up from the rear. Day Day told everyone to focus their attention on the two vehicles behind them. He then yanked out his .45 and sped ahead, against traffic, toward the flying cop car. Just as he was about 50 yards out, Day Day let off five carefully placed shots. Time seemed to slow to a crawl as the first shot pinged off of the front bumper. Then the next shot hit the windshield but missed it's mark.

Adjusting his aim appropriately, Day Day fired three consecutive shots, center mass. The first tore into the driver's neck, the second followed immediately and struck the driver's head, splattering the interior with gray brian matter, and the third and final shot skipped off of the hot hood of the vehicle. "Lucky shot," Day Day expressed to himself. Right then, the front tire blew out and Day Day had to swerve in order to avoid the hitting the out of control police vehicle.

The car rolled once and flipped onto it's side, blocking the road partially.

The two cars had nearly reached the tipped vehicle and Geno and Monster were savagely unloading on them ineffectively. T.Y. had reloaded and was emptying his entire magazine at the under belly of the tipped car. Just when Geno and Monster thought he was missing badly, the car exploded and engulfed the other two cars

in fireballs as they had simultaneously reached the downed police car.

"Aww, shit! This nigga's ill!" Day Day bellowed raucously.

Now, in the clear, they made a move as quickly as possible to get another vehicle before a helicopter was brought in. They were lucky that the officers

and agents had been unprepared for this eventuality and had grossly misunderstood and underestimated these men and this situation.

Locating a parking garage, Day Day drove into it calmly and let T.Y. out so that he could steal an older model Honda. Once he had the vehicle started, Day Day hopped into the driver's seat of the new getaway, and everyone loaded it up with the bounty that they were carrying with them. Monster contorted his face after climbing in and asked, "Why you steal this hoopty man? I see you on that bullshit."

"Ha ha, gotta stay inconspicuous, alrr Day Day laughed.

"For sure. You right," Monster replied with a hard smile.

Day Day drove to a rental agency so that he could get a car to take back to South Philly. Nigga's ain't trying to ride through the hood in no hot ass whip, Geno thought quietly. After Monster got the rental truck he wanted, theywent to a secluded area and transferred everything from the bottle to the rental.

After torching the Honda, they got on the highway just as

any other normal vehicle would have. T.Y. twisted up a blunt, Geno freaked a Black-n-Mild, and Monster complained. "I ain't fucking with West Philly no more, yo," he said, annoyed but relieved that by some stroke of a miracle they had made it out safe and sound. "Too much fuckin trouble and now we hot," he concluded.

"Hot as hell," Geno added.

"Fuck 'em! Can't nobody hold us, Yo. We get down when it's beef!" Day Day proclaimed.

"And Young T.Y. the truth, nigga. Yeah, we gonna hold you down, young bull. You proved yourself now. A. nigga can't doubt you even if he wanted to," Monster added.

"You see how the young bull was torching shit back there? He Alright, Monster," Day Day said and smiled happily.

"Beginner's luck!" Geno yelled out laughing.

"Ha ha, yeah, nigga, you was so scared, you couldn't miss!" Day Day teased.

"I think I saw the nigga shooting with his eyes closed," Monster roared chuckling.

"Aww, that's fucked up, y'all. Damn, that's how you feel, huh? Fuck it, let's go do it again then!" T.Y. said as his niggas poked fun at him.

"Naw, young bull, you win, nigga. Way to prove your gangsta. I respect it," Monster said proudly to his young hustler. He dapped his young nigga up and faced the rest of the problems that this day would bring. With the adrenaline quickly fading away, the weight of everything began to crash down, his mind began to focus on what he needed to do, and he suddenly felt tire. Exhausted.

Monster decided to call Fay and find out how it had gone

with Wyan Wyan. He was worried because he couldn't be there for her. Over the past six months, he and Fay had seemed to fall madly in love. She had been his crutch and vice versa. monster couldn't ever remember going soft over a chick before. He figured that would either be his strength or his weakness. His vision or his blindness. But Monster was smart, not easily fooled and usually a very good discerner of character. Usually.

"Hello?" Fay answered angrily.

"What's wrong, baby? Everything alright, love?" Monster asked sincerely.

"Your fucking boy E. That's what's wrong. Your good for nothing ass nigga!" Fay said hotly.

"What's up, Fay? What happened? Stop yelling and talk to me, girl. A nigga can't even hear you if you're yelling and shit."

"Listen, E. Bone Neck was supposed to help but he didn't."

"What you mean?"

"Look, after I told him to wait in the parking lot and to watch because I was going to tell Wyan outside, Bone said 'okay.' But when Wyan started yelling and pushed me down, nothing happened. He didn't get out of the car or anything. Then he grabbed me by my hair. That's when Bone Neck got out with his gun. He walked up and told Wyan to get off of me. After that he walked to the parking lot with him and even talked to him for about fifteen minutes. They shook hands before leaving, then they left. Together. Herbie Luv Bug drove Wyan's car and Wyan got in with Bone Neck. Bone pulled up to where I was watching and said, 'Tell Monster I said fuck him!' Then they rode off," Fay finished.

"What the fuck… word? Aww, it's on. It's on now. I shoulda been murked that nigga for that bullshit he pulled a while ago but fuck it. Can't cry over spilled milk. I'mma have to deal with that nigga when I get back. I'll be home in about two hours, love. Go to the house and call me when you get there. Love you."

"I love you, too, baby. Bye."

"The fuck happen?" Geno questioned with a look of curiosity, which in turn quickly dispelled and transformed into a disappointing anger when Monster responded simply.

"Bone Neck flipped. He rolling with Wyan Wyan now."

CHAPTER 10

A START TO THE END

"So what made you flip, -mid? I know Monster had you paid," Wyan Wyan prodded Bone Neck.

"Man, fuck them niggas! I'm tired of them dumb ass niggas, bah. I had a smooth deal a couple of months ago and the boy Monster ain't want me to do it. So I do it anyway, feel me? Shit, nigga, I took a couple of young soldiers with me for back up. It was a set up and two of the young niggas got killed and four of them got booked. Two made it out after a shoot out and we got the work plus the paper," Bone Neck said with a hint of pride before continuing. This nigga, Monster, get salty and put me on the block for the past almost six months! Like I'm some young paper nigga. I need big money and I know y'all boys getting it out here. So I had to come holla," Bone Neck finished with a little flattery, knowing exactly how to play these little niggas.

Truth was, he really knew they weren't getting near what he was making but he needed their pride blown up. He figured since they were so young, he could take over their established credit and foot soldiers. They would have to respect him after he helped them get rid of Monster and 7th Street, and of course, they would love him after they see what kind of connects he could bring in.

"Yeah, I feel you, Bone," Wyan began, "I would've been happy if you brought back the work and the dough, boo. How much was it?"

"A soft two mil, young bull."

"Two fuckin' million dollars?! And the nigga Monster got hot over a couple of bodies dropping and some young cats in jail? The fuck? Yeah, you came to the right place. We can do for each other, Wyan Wyan said.

"Man, fuck we gonna do about Fay and them Seventh Street niggas?" Herbie Luv Bug asked. He and Wyan had been building their army for the past six months with was, they were speaking about war with what seemed the wrong niggas to war with. They had better than an exclusive arsenal of artillery plus they had connections and alliances from other sets who would be fearful not to help 7th Street. They had heard about the intense street wars that 7th Street had produced and the damage and carnage they could inflict, but neither Wyan, Herbie, nor Bone had ever experienced that part of 7th Street.

I can't see it being that bad, thought Herbie Luv Bug. He had no earthly idea, though.

"I know y'all probably don't wanna hear this, but we can't war with them niggas. They're too deep and they're strapped in, you feel me? But I know who we can fuck with to get at them niggas real quick. You know, shake shit up a little bit," Bone Neck said, thinking of a long time acquaintance.

"Who?" Herbie asked at the same time as Wyan.

"My peoples. the Sixth Street Killas," Bone Neck responded.

"They won't even fuck with us if we're trying to get any kind of hit on Seventh Street. We already tried, boo. They ain't ready. The scared, homie," Herbie Luv Bug informed Bone as he started to smile suspiciously.

"I told you, they my peoples, nigga. but we gonna have to pay. Hard, too. The nigga, Black .a.teq need some big paper for this one," Bone Neck said.

"How much you think?" Wyan Wyan questioned intently.

"Hold up, I'mma call him," Bone Neck said as he picked up his Samsung.

"Hello? Yeah, what's up, Nate? Ya young but need one. Well, I ain't fucking with them niggas no more, so that's why I'm calling you. Plus it something to do with them lames anyway. Come on, nigga, I need this one. How much? Alright, I'mma call you and meet up with you so I can drop the paper off and give you the specs on the shit. Yeah, it's a wrap. Holla," Bone Neck said, finishing his conversation with the 6th Street Killas head nigga in charge.

Bone Neck was frustrated because he knew it was going to cost but he didn't know it would cost so much. He also knew he'd be paying alone because these young niggas could put their life savings together and probably wouldn't even cover the half now, half later policy if they tried.

"How much?" Herbie Luv Bug asked, noticing Bone's look of ill contempt. He looked green around the gills, like something was stuck in his throat. Probably the number that was the amount that it would cost them to handle the job. Surely it can't be that much, he thought. He just hoped it wasn't more than 2 or 3 hundred thousand. Even that would likely wipe him out, but it would be worth it.

I'm killing two birds with one stone on this... I gotta prove my loyalty to these lames and I get to burn them 7th Street niggas in the process, Bone Neck schemed. "Three million. Half now, half later. I got it, though," Bone Neck said calmly yet angry that his savings would be tapped nearly dry. Leaving him with only about six hundred thousand and bills to pay. His cash had been steady dwindling in light of his demotion. He was spending about three or four times what he was making because of that shit. But fuck it, thought Bone Neck, I gotta figure how much this is gonna make me, not how much I'm losing. This is a power move. At that, he smiled a smile of triumph.

"Three million?!" Wyan Wyan choked out. "Shit, ass, fuck, that's a lot of money," he finished in disbelief. At that, Bone Neck had to smile again.

"Money is my middle name," he countered with a chuckle. Damn, these niggas is broke, he thought to himself.

"What's good, T.Y.?" Monster asked as he answered his iphone.

"Ay yo, Monster, niggas came and tried to shoot the block up but we took care of shit. C-Block got his left eye knocked out by a bullet and Fat Bul got hit but he only got grazed, though. It was a flesh wound. He acting like a bitch but he Alright. We might have to fuck something up, though, young bull, because you'll never believe who we popped in the chest."

"Who?" asked a now fully awake Monster.

"George. The nigga from Sixth. Street!"

"Sixth Street? So them niggas trying to play two sides of the field, huh? Alright, I'mma show niggas for real. Ay yo, T.Y. round me up five young shooters. I need some reliable ones, nigga. Call Rafiq and tell him I said let you and my young niggas get the pretty three fifty-sevens. He'll know exactly what you're talking about. Go over there and strap up. Then we gonna meet up on Seventh Street in... umm... forty-five minutes. Peace."

"Peace."

Monster hung up the phone and picked up for another call. "Yo, get up, fool," Monster said to Geno's exhausted greeting on the other end. "Get ready. Pick up and meet me on Seventh Street in about forty-five minutes. Call Day Day and tell him the same things. Oh, don't forget the liquid band-aid. Peace."

"Holla," responded Geno, hot knowing what was going on, but trusting his boss he grabbed a few pipes, masks, gloves, and a large container of liquid band-aid. Geno brushed his teeth, twisted a blunt, and walkedjout of the door talking to Day Day over the phone.

"Sounds big. Yeah, me, too, Day Day, I does big. Peace."

CHAPTER 11

FAVOR FOR A FAVOR

Three smoke filled, well tinted, smoke filled Honda Accords crept down Snyder Avenue. The biggest main street in South Philly was now being used as an avenue that led to what was sure to become a grisly scene of mass murder.

Monster called Day Day, one car behind him. "Yo, bull, get ready. It should be about five to ten niggas out here. Let's send a message before the real favor is returned. I want everything moving, bleeding. No women and kids though. Make sure them young niggas you got with you know that. Tell them not to just be stupid shooting. See what you hit and hit what you see! Then call T.Y. behind you and tell him to relay that message to them three niggas he got in his car. No mistakes. Peace," Monster said and hung up.

"Niggas gonna talk about this, Monster," Geno started while seated behind the wheel. "You don't think that we re leaving our calling card too obviously?" He finished curiously.

"Nope. The streets know us. They also know if they talk then I'mma find out who said what," Monster stated as he looked down at his black .357 with a gold number 7 engraved in the handle and on the barrel. Not even Snoop is going to be able to pin this one on us. They're just number sevens printed on guns, you know? I mean he know, but he don't know, you dig? Fuck 'em anyway. I don't care if the muthafucka is out here when we lay this bitch down, he getting it, too. I wouldn't give a muthafuck if the sumbitch was sitting in the whip with us right now... he better get down or lay down, you feel me? Monster ranted as he held up his pistol with the golden 7s engraved on it.

"I want the streets to know who it is that did it, you know?

"Yeah, young bull, I got you. Ay yo, mask up, we about to hit the strip right now," Geno said as he pulled on his mask.

Parking at the end of the block that was called 6th Street Killas, Geno and Monster waited for T.Y to stop and put three niggas into the car with them. Afterwards, the other two cars sped up the street as if they were racing. They could see the confused looks on the faces of the street hustlers as they burned down the road. Confused but not too worried. These kinds of things went on in the hood, people raced all the time.

Once they got to the other end, they parked and Geno spun the whip around to face away from the street. Monster and Geno could make out the two cars at the far end of the street parking and chirped them, "Yo, y'all ready? Good. Y'all know what to do. Let's get it!"

Monster, Geno and the three young bulls, Quan and Zeek and Rasul ran up the street. At the same time, T.Y. Day Day, and the two young bulls they had, T.J. and Toby, hopped out of the car on their end of the block and sprinted down the street hard. All had their guns drawn. Each held a .357 completely identical to Monster's.

Geno and Monster's crew reached the 6th Street niggas first and caught them slipping. As the guns were raised, the eyebrows of the unsuspecting victims were lifted just as high.

Surprise highlighted their features as they had just mere moments to register the scene. Death awaited them and before they could even react, reach for their weapons, or even run, 'BLADDOW!' the heavy canons rang out with a deafening sound. The retort echoed off of the surrounding homes and spelled disaster to those targeted by it.

All five .357s let go their fire, dripping four of the eleven 6th Street niggas running up the street. Bullets tore through of the nigga's back and emptied his blood onto the cold pavement. His life force spilled out of him like so much kool-aid. The other three were hit by so many shells that it might not even be possible to tell how many times they were shot. Those big ass guns turned men into meat. Geno caught one more with two shots after the other three emptied their entire clips into the niggas that they dropped, leaving six still running up the street.

With empty guns, they reloaded and began letting off unaimed shots, attempting to cause a bit of confusion and fear in the running men. Right on time, came the other four from the bottom of the street and they were picking the 6th Street niggas off. They were caught between both groups of shooters and were too hassled and afraid to think of reaching for their firearms. They just wanted to live... if wishes had wings they would fly, and so would niggas who were being shot at.

The last group of niggas were gunned down without 7th Street's crew even breaking stride. After the last one went down with one in his chest and three in his back, everyone dropped their guns and kept running in the directions that they were already traveling. Monster, Geno and their three young guns took T.Y. and Day Day's cars at the top of the street while Day Day and T.Y.'s crew all hopped in Monster and Geno's ride at the bottom of the street and sped off before the police could arrive. It was the quickest 3 minute slaughter you could ever imagine. The three young guns passed Monster and Geno as they were headed to the shop to get the whips chopped.

"I can hear the news now," Geno said, "Eleven people viciously gunned down. Nine .357 magnum handguns were found on the scene, each with a gold number seven engraved on it. What does it mean? Tonight on Channel Six News," he finished as he and Monster laughed at his poor attempt to recreate a news anchor.

"You'll never get a job in t.v.," Monster said, laughing some more.

"Monster, seriously, how fucked up in the head must we be to be sitting here laughing after we just shot up eleven people, man?" Geno asked concerned with their lack of remorse.

"In order for there to be law, there must be lawlessness. In order for there to be happiness, there must be sadness. In order for there to be sanity, bull, somebody gotta be insane... who better than us?" Monster said philosophically.

CHAPTER 12

HERE WE GO!

"HERE WE GO, HERE WE GO, NIGGA! HURRY UP, MONSTER, IT'S ON," Geno yelled as Monster hustled into Geno's living room and found a spot on the sofa next to T.Y.

"Turn it up," Day Day said. he was enthusiastic, grinning like a kid on Christmas, or his birthday. The smile he wore was a classic, stretching from ear to ear, coloring his face in a bright childlike joy. But for all the wrong reasons.

...and our main story today here on Channel Six News is..." reported the thin faced Ken Barbie on tv. He seemed to make eye contact with Monsteras he spoke about this late breaking top story.

Why do they always have to look like Barbie Dolls just to tell the fucking news, Monster wondered.

Ken Barbie continued, "Earlier today, a vicious cycle of events took place as eleven men were murdered on Philadelphia's south side. Young men in the age range of eighteen to twenty-seven were gunned down by an unknown number of assailants. Witnesses report multiple men, however, we have not confirmed the exact count.

Police report that nine, count that, nine three fifty-seven magnum handguns were found on the scene. Each firearm had a gold number seven engraved onto it. What does it mean?"

At this revelation, Geno began to yell, "I told you, nigga, I told you what they was going to say, Monster! Almost exactly what I said in the whip, remember? That shit is crazy, young bull"

"Yeah, you hit that shit on the head, but shut the fuck up with your big ass

Dumbo ears. I'm trying to hear this!" Monster responded leaving Geno looking goofy.

"Names are not being released until the victims' families are notified and each person can be identified. Still in chock, the city weeps at this drastic loss. Police Homicide Detective and lead officer on the case is set to address the public... Lets now go Live".

"Snoop?" T.Y. said. "What this bitch ass nigga got to say? He don't know shit," he declared vehemently.

"Shh, nigga, he on," Day Day said silencing him.

"...and when we find out who's murdering our city's innocent youths, we're going to get you... you... you monsters! That's what you are for killing innocent young men. You're monsters!" Snoop said menacingly into the news camera and microphone at the press conference.

Monster listened intently at Snoops shout out to him. Monster knew that Snoop was talking to him, even if the press didn't. No matter, though, he can't prove shit! Monster reminded himself casually.

"You know he was talking to you, man," Day Day commented knowingly. "He hate you."

"I know. Fuck Snoop! I run South Philly! I built this shit from the ground up. Me and y'all niggas did this. Niggas fuck with Seven Street this is what happens. I'm bringing hell to the streets if niggas wanna test. And it ain't over. We ain't finished with Sixth Street yet. But we will be... soon," Monster said angrily pulling on the kush he was smoking.

"You need some anger management classes, Monster," Young T.Y. said as they all cracked up laughing. Then more seriously, "So, why them niggas come after us 711 anyway.

"Shit, I don't know, somebody had to pay them niggas, T.Y." Monster explained.

"But who, Monster? Them niggas know that it ain't no money worth what we can bring. They was around when we was wiping niggas out for looking at us wrong. It was more than money, Monster. Maybe money plus something else," Geno said airing his opinion.

"Alright," Monster began, "T.Y. find out what you can about this shit and keep a hammer with you, 'cause them niggas ain't all dead. Day Day and Geno, y'all know what to do. I'm tired. We got work to do tomorrow. I'm going home. Fuck y'all niggas, I'm sleepy. Ha ha! But for real, though, hit me on the hip if y'all come up with something. Geno, get some new heat for us. Heavy shit. Not too heavy though. I know you, nigga. Fuck around and slide through with a rocket launcher or some other shit like that. Anyway, niggas, I'm tapped, so I'll holla. Peace." Monster said as he dapped his niggas up and left to go home. He checked his .357 before he left. Locked and stocked.

"What the fuck?!" Wyan Wyan exclaimed watching t.v. "Bone Neck, look at this shit. You said this shit was gonna be cool. Eleven niggas? The same day, nigga? At the same time...

NIGGA?! And they got away? Bul, this that bullshit right here, and now we gonna have Seventh Street and Sixth Street at our throats. What the fuck?"

"First off, Wyan, Sixth Street operates under their own policy. If they get in shit on a contract, Nate knows that it ain't our fault. He gotta take care of that shit. Second, I told you Monster don't play no games. I knew this shit was gonna happen," Bone Neck said.

"So why the fuck you hire them niggas for three fucking million if they couldn't handle the job? That's fucking stupid, Tone! Wyan said.

Wyan sighed. He pinched the bridge of his nose in frustration, trying to ease the building headache that seemed to be coming to him more and more as of late from dealing with these young simple ass niggas who didn't seem to know much of anything about being a real gangster. His patience was being tried, but he knew that he would have to somehow summon up some more if he was going to be successful with his plan and have to deal with these young suckers in the process.

"We had to take the attention off of us, Wyan. Plus, now Seventh Street gonna have to war against two sets instead of one. It makes it a little more equal. And we know that he doesn't even know he's at war with us yet. All he probably thinks is that I switched because I was salty," Bone Neck said.

"Alright, bull, it's your money. Just let me know what the next move is," Wyan Wyan said anxiously.

"Then next one is big, Wyan. Real big. I'm talking big on some dinosaur type shit. Get the soldiers ready. It's almost time, buiz," Bone Neck replied with a smirk on his face. See, I am smart. You ain't ready for this one, Monster. Won't be long now... won't be long at all, Bone Neck thought to himself.

CHAPTER 13

WHICH WAR?

"Hey, baby," Monster called as he strolled into the house. Fay sat on the couch in front of the t.v. frowning. "What's wrong, love?" Monster asked concerned.

"El don't 'what's wrong' me! You know what's been on t.v. all day? Huh? You did that shit, didn't you?" Fay asked with contempt in her tone.

"I plead the fifth," Monster said mockingly.

"What the fuck is wrong with you? How could you do some shit like that? I ain't gonna be having that shit while I'm up in here. Who you think you is, boy? Al Capone or something? You know what, it don't even matter. One thing is true, though. You gonna have to quit this killing shit, Fay demanded almost as if she had planned her speech.

Monster was beside himself. She must not know who she talking to. Either that or I'm getting soft out here, he thought angrily. As the volcano that was his temper began to let off steam, he reacted. "First off, Fay, I been in this game damn near eleven years. I been on top of this city for damn near six. I do what the fuck I want, when the fuck I want! Nobody, 000h bitch, I mean nobody, regulate my moves! I'm muthafucking Monster. Now, I was gonna smack the shit out you for talking to me crazy like that. But I said naw... bitch I said naw. But let me give your ass this thought. I been doing this a lot longer than I known you. You might think that everything is peaches and fucking cream but it ain't I made millions doing what you think I did today. And I'm gonna keep my millions doing what you think I did today. Don't like it? Leave. Don't let the door knob hit ya where the good Lord split ya. Learn to deal with it or deal without it. Don't you ever tell me what to do again, unless you telling me to drop my damn pants 'cause you planning to suck the color off a nigga dick. Until then, this my shit. Worry about your shit," Monster relayed with venom and anger cycling through him.

Fay b%. an to cry and apologize to Monster because she knew she was about to fuck up. That's wasn't what she wanted. Everything had to go smooth for her. She needed this to work out. Monster laid her down and accepted her apology.

Early the next morning, Monster picked up his phone and dialed Geno's number. "Yo, what it do, man?" Tell everybody to meet up at your spot in an hour. You got that? Good, aught, I'll holla. Peace."

"Where you going:" Fay questioned with the same tone she'd taken with him last night. Monster shot her a look so vicious she gasped and left it alone. Fay was on the phone when Monster got out of the shower. She hadn't known he was out because he still had a habit of leaving the water running.

She was whispering angrily into the receiver, whe she saw

him she guiltily hung up the phone and said, "Baby, do you want breakfast?" in a sweet little tone.

"Now she thinks I'm stupid, Monster contemplated. Must be fucking someone else. I'll catch her. This is my city. I know everything, thought Monster as he dressed and walked out the door silently... to his block, 7th Ditkean Street.

"Y'all niggas ready?" Monster asked Geno., Day Day, and T.Y. as he walked into Geno's condo.

"Ay yo, you straight, Monster?" Geno questioned, noticing Monster. He looked as if someone had shit in his shoes.

"Yeah, bull, let's go take care of this shit. Then, we gonna kick it again tonight. I see you fitted, Young T.Y. You pieced up, huh, young bull?" Monster Joked with him. He had really begun dressing and stunting since Monster gave him a cool quarter mil for that West Philly shit.

"Yeah, you know, Monster. I gotta stay fly and high!"...he declared with a chuckle.

All four wore ankle length Saint Taurent trench coats lined and fitted with a sawed off twelve gag-e Mossberg pump shotgun. Day Day and T.Y. wore midnight blue suits while Monster and Geno were donned in black, for the funeral. They took a silent ride across town with grim determination in their hearts. You could always tell when someone was about to die. The day just always seemed to have a dark feel about it. And this particular day was darker than most.

Day Day opened the door to the apartment building and uppercutted the lights out of the first person he saw. The man took the punch similar to how he would have take a sledgehammer to the chin. The crunching blow smashed his features and lifted him off his feet, depositing him onto the ground like a sack of grain.

His head lolled to the side and his tongue hung from his thin lips, slack out of his broken jaw. He was asleep, snoring like a bear.

When others, surprised, approached, he yanked out his shotty and T.Y. stepped through the door with his out and up. While they stood guard over the front entrance and held the niggas at bay, they made them strip and lay on the floor next to their broken jawed cohort. Geno and Monster went up the stairs to the apartment they were looking for.

Not bothering to knock, Geno kicked open the door and went into the bedroom where Nate was jumping up at the sound of the splintering wood from Geno's legged assault. Geno and Monster entered the room and raised their pumps like a salute to the flag so Nate wouldn't budge. He surely has a tool in here somewhere, Geno thought knowingly.

There was a girl, naked, in the bed with Nate. She started to scream until Geno shut her up by pointing his Mossberg at her. Monster finally came to terms with what he was seeing and spoke first.

"How old are you, girl?"

"Thirteen," she stammered in response. And it wasn't hard to tell either. Especially by judging her facial appearance. She still had that innocent child's face, that fresh and fleshy baby fat that comes only with youth. She looked afraid. Afraid as if she were about to die next to this slob of a man with whom she shared a bed.

"What your young ass doing here fucking with this old ass nigga?" Geno lept in, questioning her.

"He said he would give me twenty dollars

"Get up and put your clothes on," Monster said in a powerful voice, disgusted. After she was dressed, Monster said, "Take care of her, Geno."

At that she began to cry and beg for her life. Nate looked confused because he know, everyone knew, that Monster didn't kill innocent women or children, at least not purposefully. And this girl was both, child and woman.

"Stop all that damn crying, girl. Shit, women are too sensitive," Geno affirmed as he handed her a bankroll of about five bands. "Take this and go down the stairs and holla at my two young bulls. They holding pumps like these, so don't sneak up on them. They have itchy trigger fingers. They'll tell you what they want you to do. Oh, and forget what and who you saw here today, okay?" Geno said.

She nodded her agreement and before she left, hocked a fat loogie and spit it in Nate's face. He must had forgotten who was in the room because he tried to jump up out of the bed and get the little girl, but Geno's shotgun butt met his face with a resounding smack and sat him back down on his bed dazed and bloodied.

"Aww, shit," Nate said, his eyes nearly rolling around to the back of his head. He looked to nearly go into unconsciousness and that wasn't what they wanted.

"Tighten up, nigga! You know what's up," Monster began. "Tell me what I wanna know."

"Monster, man, I know you want to kill me but I was on contract," Nate said.

"Fuck outta here," Geno started. "Fat bitch, who were you working for?"

His bulk jiggled, and the smell coming from him was

unghastly. Sweat was beading on his forehead, though whether it was from the exertion of putting his dick inside of the little girl or from the nervousness of having multiple shotguns pointing in his direction, no one could be sure. Possibly it was from a little of both. Nate was fat, black, and ugly as ever, however, he stayed Gucci down to his socks. He looked nothing like Biggie Smalls, though. Neither could he rap a bar. It seemed his only talents involved taking assassination hits on people and fucking children. Bad combination.

"Damn, y'all, you know I don't be releasing my contacts all like that... Nate started but was cut short by another gun butt to the face. This time it was Monster's.

"Mutha' bitch fucka', don't make me kill your fat ass. And I'll make for sure that I take it real slow. This is your building, so you know ain't nobody calling no cops, nigga," Monster finished.

"Monster, you gonna kill me anyway,"Black Nate said knowingly.

"For what? Bidness is bidness, nigga. You wanted some paper. I mean it was stupid, got a few of your niggas dead, but I can't hate' you for your love of money. So, I'm not going to kill you for taking a contract out on me, as long as it doesn't happen again. Besides, I killed eleven of your young niggas. Call it even," Monster said matter-of-factly.

Now Geno began to stare intently at Monster because Monster never went back on his word. EVERYONE knew that. Including Nate.

"Oh, word? You gonna look out for me like that, Monster? You good peoples for that. I'mma honor your word man. Look, bull, it was Bone Neck and Wyan Wyan's clique. Them young

Fifth Street niggas. They ain't want me to go after you. They said to hit some young block runner named T.Y. but it was still me fucking with your set, so I charged him three million. And you know I don't usually take out a hit on you man. I would never... except that Bone Neck is my cousin, bull. Not too many people know that, though. He said y'all was tripping on him and that you wouldn't even find out, man. I swear I didn't--"

"Give me the money he paid you, nigga," Monster demanded.

"I only got half because the job wasn't finished but it's in the safe inside of that closet. It's open, too," Nate said teary eyed. One-point-five millie for my life? Well worth it, he thought to himself resolutely.

Geno took the bags of money out of the vault like safe and Monster put down his Mossberg.

Nate sighed a breath of relief just as Monster reached to his hip holster and yanked out his .357 Smith and Wesson. He shot Nate in the thigh, the fat leg took the powerful blast the way a watermelon would have. Not well. There was no way it could have contained that explosion of power from such a close quarters. He looked down in complete surprise as he realized that his entire leg was now separated... the bone and blood were everywhere. Nearly faintin he said, "Awww, you said... you said..." Nate stammered, going into shock.

"This is for what your fat stank ass did with that little ass girl, muthafucka," Monster said answereing the question that died on Nate's lips. "Bitch nigga, she was thirteen!"

'BOOM BOOM!' The canon was ringing out as Monster started letting loose on Nate. At that Geno picked up his pump, backed slowly out of the room and began pumping slug after slug into the carcass in front of him.

They must be fucking that nigga up good," T.Y. said as he heard the commotion coming from upstairs. there were four niggas on the floor. "You know what to do. Monster said, 'as soon as you hear us shooting, kill them of butt booty ass naked niggas,' " he said in finality.

"Yup," Day Day responded. "Yup."

"Come on, let's peel," Monster said to Geno after they heard the gun blasts coming from the downstairs lobby. After running through the dismembered and shredded bodies lying in what seemed like a lake of blood, they got into the car that T.Y. was pulling up in.

Geno relayed the incident to Day Day and T.Y. about the contracts after T.Y. told them that they'd sent the girl off before the gun shots.

"Bone Neck think he smart, y'all," Monster stated. "He wanted to throw us off balance with this move and try some sneak attak Pearl Harbor shit. But we gonna take real good care of them niggas asap!"

CHAPTER 14

MURDER WAS THE CASE

Monster was just tired. That's all. He just wanted to sleep. What he didn't know was, that was about to change. It seemed to him that it was the beginning of another war. This one was more easy than any of his prior battles but still dangerous all the same. Bullets could catch you anywhere, at anytime, and they could come from anyone. Boy, did he fail to really grasp that one.

Monster opened his door and stopped short as soon as it swung open. Pulling out his tre pound, he looked into the living room and saw that it was trashed. It looked as if an earthquake had hit. Or a tornado, for that matter. Broken glass was flitted about the floor from the expensive oak coffee table. Couches were overturned and holes were cut into the fabric. That on3is Fay's favorite, he thought to himself.

FAY! "Oh shit," he cursed silently as he realized that she might or rather likely was in the condo when whatever this was had occurred. He disarmed the security system. It had begun chiming as soon as he cracked the door. Monster went from room to room looking for his woman.

He went into the master bathroom and saw the message written to him across the mirror. "Your move now. Move wrong and she dies. Keep your cell on. Call you later, sweetie!" It was written in Fay's lipstick in large scratchy handwriting. Monster heard sirens that seemed to be approaching his place and he ran to his safe. there were bullet dents in it and shell casings on the floor. An obvious break-in attempt No haps, though, that safe if top of the line, he pondered as he opened it and tossed in his .357 along with the twenty bands he had on him.

He had stopped by the incinerator that one of his buildings housed and tossed in the bloody garments from earlier and changed before he got home. He never expected the next turn of events. For that fact, he would never expect anything that was soon to come about.

Monster was about to be at war with an enemy that he couldn't see and one that had raised the stakes by the kidnapping of his woman. This would test his resolve, his experience, and all of the time that he had put into the game.

"Freeze!" the officer yelled as he rushed into Monster's place, followed by four other cops.

"Fucking cops. This my shit," Monster spewed with his hands still hanging by his sides. His mood was sour and his face had a defiant set to it, it appeared to be chisled from stone, his voice tainted with fire. "And I ain't call na'an one of y'all sumbitches. I hate police anyway. Get out!" He clamored in a deafening tone that brooked no argument.

The patrolmen already on the scene were visibly shaken. "You didn't need to, Monster.

Were here to protect and serve, remember Philadelphia Police, at your service," said Snoop, filing in the room after the last officer had come in. "You have the right to remain silent..."

"What you doing? This my shit, nigga. How you gonna try and arrest me?" Monster demanded, irate.

After Snoop finished reading Monster his Miranda rights, he was cuffed and Snoop decided to toy with him. "I got your black ass now, boy."

"I ain't did shit... boy," Monster countered.

"Oh, well, I guess you weren't informed by your precious streets, then? You're under arrest for your involvement with the deaths of federal agents, two young boys, and for running a criminal organization that was connected to the incident nearly six months ago. Sound familiar? We couldn't get your little fucking runners to talk but I got one better. An eye witness," Snoop said with a disfigured smile upon his face. And with that, the uniformed officers led Monster away to his chariot.

"Mr. Moore this is not good," said the beautiful Rodnieka. She was Monster's high priced lawyer who happened to be a fox outside of the courtroom and a wolf when inside. "The young guys who got locked up did not roll on you. However, the state says that they have eyewitness testimony on this incident. The witness apparently has information and confessions about a number of other murders you were a leading party in. But he won't release this information until his conditions are met, which I'm sure they will be. They've got a hard on so big for you, they may be willing to fuck everything just to get the tip in you. Right now, it's still a state case, but I'm sure the feds aren't far behind. They 11 be here soon to get you if they can get this witness to talk," she said finishing her statement.

"What terms? What this nigga want for his end of the bargain Nieka?",'Monster asked reluctantly, not sure he really even wanted to know what Bone Neck had sold his soul for.

"Complete immunity," she stated plainly.

"What?! They gonna give it to him? For murdering feds?" Monster was beside himself, he was incredulous.

"Well, he claims that he was brainwashed by you and you gave him the type of money that he needed for his family to survive. A family that you threatened to murder if he didn't do exactly as you told him to. Plus, he claims your empire was so strong that he feared you and the police because you have some of them on your payroll as well. They're not releasing his name to us for obvious reasons," she replied.

"I know who it is. I know exactly," said Monster matter-of-factly.

"Your bail is set for one million dollars, Mr Moore, cash assured!" the judge called out angrily, as if he had accomplished a major feat, giving Monster a bond he thought he couldn't hope to make.

Monster thanked the judge, rather smugly, and turned to face Geno in the rear of the courtroom. Geno nodded to Monster, he knew he'd be be out of jail in a few hours or so. He'd been in jail for the past week waiting for the arraignment. He was issued a "No Bond" initially, so he was waiting for his indictment, which he had gotten yesterday. He was more than ready to go home after spending more than a couple of minutes in the CFCF county jail.

Damn, he thought to himself, that's got to be the worst county jail in the world. Pay your bond and sit for four more fucking hours!

Geno wasn't waiting for him outside as he expected, but shortly before he was about to ask a nearby person if he could use their cellphone, a Lexus pulled up. The candy coated 1500 skirted up with jackhammer base and jurassic size chrome rims. Monster knew it was T.Y. and he hustled over into the whip.

"What's good, young bull?" Monster exclaimed, happy to be out.

"Shi-i-i-t, nigga, what's poppin, bull?" imma take you to the crib because Geno and Day Day out making moves, you dig? You know, holding down the fort." T.Y. informed.

"Yeah I know. I know." Monster said. Then, because he didn't write from jail or use the phones, because he couldn't and wouldn't trust them, he explained everything his lawyer had said, even though he was pretty sure she had relayed everything his lawyer had said.

"So, what, you think it was Bone Neck. don't you?' T.Y. asked as he guided the luxury vehicle over Philly's battered city streets.

"You know it. How my house look?" Monster asked remembering the mess he had come home to a little over a week ago.

"Geno put your shit back together real nice like. Plus, I dropped off a gift for you. Stop looking at me like that, you'll see it when you get there. I ain't telling you. No, for real, Monster, stop looking at me like that," he said grinning as he passed Monster the half smoked blunt of purple kush that he had in the car.

"Bet not be no muhfuckin' surprise party bullshit neither, bull. I got work to do, and you know they kidnapped Fay," Monster said.

"I don't know," T.Y. said unsure.

"How you don't know, T.Y.? I thought you said the streets be mad talking?"

"I'm just saying, I don't know, Monster. I don't know," T.Y. said to his boss, hoping that his gift would cheer him up and take his mind off of things for at least a little while.

"You coming up, T.Y.?" Monster asked as they pulled into his parking area.

"Naw, I got shit to do," he smirked. "Just have a fun time with your gift, young bull." More. smirking.

"Yo, you weird, nigga," Monster said with a smile.

"Yeah, I hear you, it's been a week, you got a lot built up. Be easy," T.Y. broke into hysterical laughter and Monster smiled and told him that he was gay for acting so strange. Obviously, this was a private joke between T.Y. and his own self.

"Whatever, T.Y." Monster chuckled. "Peace."

"I'll holla," T.Y. nodded. They dapped up and Monster went to his front door.

Monster looked down at his feet and noticed that he now had a door mat. Door mats are gay, he thought with a chuckle. Someone-Geno-must have bought it. He mouthed the words printed on it to himself silently. "Welcome Home."

CHAPTER 15

WELCOME HOME

Monster unlocked the door and once he got the audible 'CLICK', he swung it open. He could see his patio blinds were open, revealing the setting sun. It was nearly dark outside and Monster was tired. He felt like he had been hit with a bag of bricks while walking up a mountain. He hadn't slept well in a hot week. He felt dirty and he was hungry. Mostly, though, he was horny. Damn, he thought, to himself. Fay is gone. He felt bad for needing some pussy while she was in despair, but fuck, I'm only human, he thought. I just got to wait till them niggas call and tell me what they want.

He was undressing in his bedroom and about to get into the shower when his mind began to tell him how much he wanted to fuck. Then his dick began to tell him as well. Ah, fuck it, I'm going to get some poontang after I get out of this water.

He got into the hot shower, which was really needed, and cleaned like never before. Geno knocked on Monster's door. "He either sleep or in the shower," T.Y. said. "We better hope he in the shower."

"He is. If I know him like I think I do, it's going to be a long one, too," Geno said as he slipped his key into Monster's door. Sure enough, the shower was running. Geno stopped to admire his work on the living room. Gorgeous, he thought, better than before.

He rolled the cart into Monster's bedroom. He placed the bucket of ice and four bottles of Rose on it. Next to that, a bowl with a quarter pound of kush and tent already twisted blunts along with a large box of unopened swishers.

T.Y. plugged his MP3 player into the stereo and selected his "Slow Jams" playlist in Monster's room and turned it on softly. They put his gifts on the bed and unwrapped them, smirking and giggling like little school girls. They walked out.

Monster was hopping out of the shower and turned off the water. First time in forever that I did that, he thought with a laugh. He was still thinking of which chicken he was going to call to serve him when he heard the sounds from his bedroom. They wafted to his ears and piqued his interest and also grated on his sense of caution. There should not be any sounds coming from his bedroom.

What is that? Music? He wrapped his towel around his waist and went into his bedroom. His smile told the whole story. "A gift, huh?" he muttered at the sight of the two naked women on his bed. They were taunting him, touching on each other and licking their lips seductively.

Damn, Monster thought, these broads is built like brick houses. He dropped his towel and went to the cart. Before popping a bottle and sparking a blunt, he read the card to himself. They're clean... and they can't get pregnant... have fun!

Monster watched the two women suck on one another's

titties. One was brown skinned, the other, a yellow bone. Then he finished reading the card. "Mooch. e and Ilia— it doesn't matter which is which! You're visiting Brazil and Cuba tonight. They're ready for you to CUM inside their borders... T.Y. and Geno. 7th Street Forever!"

Monster was draining a bottle of Rose and smoking the blunt when Moochie or T., it doesn't matter which, began sucking the fucking fuck out of his dick. This is one of the true great cocksuckers, he thought with a smile. Then the other one took over and she was better, if that was even possible. This is the other true great cocksucker, Monster reasoned playfully in his own mind. Once Monster was done with the alcohol and chronic, he jumped into the bed with Moochie and Tia... I've got to be harder than I've ever been in my life, he thought as he felt the weight of himself increase with blood flow.

Monster used to love Sesame Street as a kid and when he got older, he nicknamed his dick after himself and a character from the show. He called it the Nookie Monster. He knew it was corny but the thought of it always made him laugh because he could imagine it screaming, "NOOOkiieee!!!! Yum yum yum!" He laughed out loud and bent Moochie or Tia over, it doesn't matter which, and plunged deeply into her. He pounded the shit out of her, releasing a bunch of stress with each stroke. She was moaning and screaming until Moochie, or Tia, it doesn't matter which, laid spread eagle in front of her and and the girl he was smashing put her face to the place. They switched a few times and Monster had his fun with them for a few more hours. He eventually exhausted himself and emptied his tank, and the girls left. He slept like a baby.

That night, Monster had a dream about the Cookie Monster.

He had gotten all of the cookies he wanted. Except one. He couldn't find his favorite cookie. Somebody had stolen it. He was angry.

CHAPTER 16

EVERYBODY FALLS

"Hello?" Monster said as he answered the phone sleepily. He felt like he had a mouth full of cotton. Cotton that had been dipped in shit and then covered in motor oil. His breath probably smelled like weed, liquor, and pussy. His three favorite things next to money. He smiled at the revelation.

"What's good, playboy?" responded the familiar voice of Geno on the other end. Then continuing, "You had fun, niggerachie?"

"Hell yeah, bruh, them bitches was all like that, bull! Damn she could suck a mean one!" Monster proclaimed, coming alive.

"Who, Moochie or Tia" Geno asked.

"It doesn't matter which!" Monster laughed hysterically as Geno joined in.

"Yeah, I know, I know," Geno chuckled. "So what... ay yo, hold up, my line beeping."

While on hold, Monster began to miss Fay more and more. His anger was building up about it. He couldn't remember the last time a nigga set his mouth to even talk ill about 7th Street, and now niggas is completely disrespecting the damn organization. I got this case, Fay gone, and Bone Neck bitch ass done flipped. "Damn, what the fuck else can go wrong?" he asked himself. Just then, Geno clicked back over...

"Yeah, my bad, Monster, that was Day Day on my other line."

"Shit, don't worry about it, nigga. What he talking about, anyway?" Monster asked.

"A nigga just wanna know what's cracking with getting them niggas back. Sowhat's good, nigga? It's going down or what, Monster? Geno asked ready for action.

"Yeah, yeah, we got it, bull. How many thangs you got?" Monster questioned.

"Shit, ummm..." Geno thought for a second. "I got two forty bangers, three SK's, three Aks, a couple of thottys and I just copped this Uzi from a nigga.

Plus, I got four tests, some Kevlar face gear, and gloves, young bull," Geno finished proudly. He loved being the armsman. He had always had connections in regard to purchasing legal and illegal firearms. There was no one more connected than Geno, no one more skilled at finding the type of ammunition and weapons necessary to win any type of war in the streets.

"Damn!" Monster started. "What you doing, starting a fucking army, but?!"

"Aww, young bull you know a nigga gots to stay strapped," Geno replied emphatically.

"Check this out," Monster said, "I think we got enough off of your stock alone, but look, tell Day Day to get ready, start moving niggas. Its about to be a wipeout. Niggas done forgot who the fuck Monster is, they done forgot how to respect Seventh Street. I'mma start jogging niggas' memory now!" Monster exclaimed angrily.

"No doubt, bull, shit let's get... oh, who the fuck?!"

"What, nigga? You aiight, Geno?"

"Hold up, Monster, hold on. It's some niggas..."

"G? Geno!"

"Yeah, nigga, I'm bout to fuck niggas up... 'CLACK CLACK'... niggas is crazy for coming here, Monster!"

"Geno, what the fuck is going on, bull?" Monster asked, hysterical about his friend. He didn't know what was going on until he'd heard it. He knew that Geno had cocked a gun on the other end but he didn't know why. Then he did. He realized what was happening once he heard the gun blasts through the receiver.

There was automatic gunfire as well as the sounds from semi auto pistols firing. 'BOOM BOOM!' 'TAT TAT TTTAATAOOOOWWW!' "Ow, shit!" Geno called out.

Monster heard his homie's painful scream and figured the phone had gotten dropped in the melee. "Ay, Geno, pick up the phone, nigga!"

Then he heard Geno again. "Hey! What you doing here? Man, dont..."

'BOOM BOOM BOOM!' Those were the last sounds that Monster heard on his end. Period.

Monster threw the phone down and was running to grab his heater when the phone rang again. "Hello?!" he screamed anxiously into the receiver. He was half hoping that it would be Geno calling to tell him. that everything was and would be alright. Instead, it was the last person he needed to be hearing anything from right now.

"Yo, what it do, killa?" Bone Neck said from the other end, grating on Monster and baiting him into a fury.

It worked. Monster exploded, "Ol' bitch ass nigga, I'mma...

"Shut the fuck up, nigga, unless you want a dead bitch!" Bone Neck retorted, cutting Monster off mid-stride.

Monster calmed himself, just barely, as his temper was fuming while Bone Neck began to speak again.

"Look, nigga, you know what time it is. I need some cake, Monster, and Fay need you to give it to me or you know what's gone shake. I'mma need like five millie, nigga. That's F-I-V-E, just in case your hoe ass can't understand. Yeah, nigga, and we just dealt with your fuck boy, Geno. Dead niggas tell no tales, right? Get that fish dinner for me and then I'mma hit you back. Keep your celly on, dickhead. Not like I gotta tell you anyway, bitch," Bone Neck said hanging up his end with a glorified smile.

Monster was lost. He was in shock. he called Day Day and T.Y. and told them to meet him up atil Geno's. he cried all the way there. When he--pulled up, the coroner's ambulance was rolling a body with a bloody sheet cast over it into the rear of the vehicle. Monster hopped out of the Benz and ran over.

"He's gone," the female paramedic stated absently to Monster as he ran up.

"Don't you fucking tell me that shit. Don't you ever fucking say no stupid shit like that again!" Monster was so sick from the thought of Geno's murder that he didn't notice T.Y. and Day Day dragging him away.

"Chill, nigga, he might make it. Cool out, yo! Damn, what

the fuck, Monster. Breathe nigga!" Day Day called into his ear.

"The fuck you mean?! Nigga, you see that sheet over his head! You see all that fucking blood? He gone, man. He gone, he..." Monster was saying before Day Day open hand slapped the shit out of him. He just looked empty eyed at Day Day. Not with the anger of a boss who killed niggas for speaking down on him, but with the empty glaze of a man dejected.

T.Y. jumped in once Monster finally quieted, Monster, that ain't Geno under the sheet. They life flighted him out of here like ten minutes ago."

Monster began to collect himself at that bit of information. All he knew was that the lady had said "he's gone." He had no idea that she meant that he was gone, as in gone to the hospital, not gone as in dead. He felt stupid. "How bad, yo?" he inquired.

"Don't know, yet. He was leaving when we got here. T.Y., push my whip, I'mma drive Monster, aiight?" Day Day half asked and half ordered.

"Alright, than. Peace, Monster, I'll see you at the hospital. Oh, and I won't even tell nobody that I seen you get slapped," T.Y. said trying to lighten the mood a bit.

"Shut up, nigga," Monster responded half smiling. "Day Day, don't slap me no more," he said, this time in full laughter.

While they sat in the waiting area at Jefferson Hospital, Monster ran down the day's events to the both of them. After about the second hour, Detective Johnson showed up.

"Already in shit and ain't been on the street twenty-four hours, huh, Mr. Moore?" he said smugly.

"Fuck you, dick lick. Fuck you want?" Monster spat, in no mod for games with Snoop. He was in rare form. It was bar none time.

"Watch your mouth, boy. It looks like you picked the wrong set to fuck with this time, huh, buddy? Got your fucking boy all shot up. Your girl all kidnapped and shit. You're fucking up, man. I thought you owned the streets, fuckhead? Who's the baller now whoardie? I heard that line in a movie once... ha ha. But this aint no movie, shitty boo boo. You're losing touch. You can't win, leave it alone," Snoop said as he got up to walk away.

"Fuck you, Snoop," Monster said. "I got something for that ass. I'll catch up to you, though," he finished.

"Whatever, Monstate," Snoop called over his shoulder as he sauntered away. "I'm a cop. You can't even handle some street niggers. How do you expect to deal with me? Till next time, asshole."

Monster was fuming. Boiling. Exploding. Noticing his composure failing, Day Day spoke up.

"Cool down, young bull. You know what we built. I'll go take care of that sucka duck right now if you want me to. you know me, nigga. Cops bleed just like the rest of us. That's my motto, baby.

"Naw, bull, not yet. We gonna get 'pm though. Some shit ain't right. I need to figure things out," Monster said as he glanced at T.Y. who was silent. He had something to say and Monster knew it. "Go ahead, T.Y. holla at me my young gun. Whatever it is, look at what's happening now. It can't be that bad."

"I don't know, Monster. Shit, its probably just some bullshit, anyway," T.Y. said resolutely.

"Come on nigga. What you scared for? You was a killer yesterday. Holla at ya nigga, NIGGA! Out with it," Monster said in a fatherly tone.

"Alright, Alright, Monster," he began. "First, I'mma say that me and Day Day and Geno all love you, so it's on you what I'm about to say. You got to figure shit out on your own," he said as Day Day shifted in his seat. He had no idea what T.Y. was about to say. he didn't like the sound of the shit, though.

T.Y. continued, "Streets still.. talking, bull. We got a leak, Monster," he said.

"I know that, nigga! I told you that Bone Neck is..."

"No," T.Y. said cutting him off. "No. Another leak. Somebody else is talking to the cops. Somebody else is fucking with Wyan Wyan and Bone Neck," T.Y. informed solemnly.

"Well, shit, T.Y., find the young nigga. Freeze his monkey ass or bring 'an to me or Day Day and..."

"No," again breaking Monster's sentence and train of thought. T.Y. continued once more. "No. It's not a young'un. It's somebody close to the top. At the top, even. It either me or Day Day, or.., I don't know."

"What?!" Monster said in apparent disgust. "I ran this shit for more than ten fucking years with these niggas. And you gonna tell me that one of 'em is snitchin' shit out? They make millions because of me, young bull. I make millions because of them," Monster had tears in his eyes. He didn't want to believe that it had come down to this, but shit was coming together with this bit of news coming into his perspective. he loved his niggas with all of his heart and that type of treachery would break his spirit in two.

"Monster, I'm just telling you what I hear. And what I think I believe. Shit is coming from a close connect. Bone Neck didn't even know you just moved. So how he know where to snatch Fay from? Geno had just moved too, right? How they know where to get him? You gotta look at that shit from the right angles, bull," T.Y. said, "You can't look with your heart, Monster. You have to look with your mind, with your logic, and with your reason. We have to keep our emotions out of it because, usually, what you want to see is what you will see." T.Y. finished.

Day Day had a crazy ass look on his face. He couldn't believe it either. At least it seemed like he didn't beleive it.

"Yeah, I think you're right, when you put it to me like that," Monster as much as admitted, reluctantly. "The nigga did say 'what you doing here?' right before that last gunshot. He would have expected Bone because he is the one that flipped. But he was never expecting whoever else that was. Damn, yo, my fucking set. Why?" Monster eyed Day Day and T.Y. He was about to start asking questions when the doctor came over to them.

CHAPTER 17

MORE FAVORS

"Hello?" the funny looking whit Nike in the Doctors coat said. "I'm Doctor Nyke."

Instantly this drew a chuckle from all three. Ironic, Monster thought.

"I take it that you're all friends or family of our patient? Yes? Okay, well, here's what we have. It's very complicated. he took five shots from two separate weapons. Three from one and two from another. He was hit once in the abdomen, twice in the chest, once in his right thigh, and I'm sorry to say, but he took a slug to the head." This last remark brought gasps and tears to all three. Silent, angry, vengeful tears.

"I would like to express to you all my apologies in this tragedy and we have lost him about three times during surgery. He's a fighter but after this last time he didn't revive. Once again, I'm sorry too..."

A nurse had come running out from some attached corridor, yelling, "Dr. Nyke! Dr. Nyke! O-R ten, scat!" It was also being paged over the loud speaker in the hospital.

"Stay here!" He said as he ran away with the nurse. All three were in confusion and silent remorse as they mourned the loss of their friend.

All Monster could think about was that one of them, T.Y., Day Day or Geno himself had caused this. Why did he ask us to stay here? he wondered to himself. Oh, the thought came to him, we have to identify the body.

After another two hours, the same doctor came back smiling. "Fuck he smiling at," Day Day snapped, irritated.

"Okay, fellas, sorry about that wait, guys," the White Nike said still smiling. "There have been a lot of drastic events and turns that have taken place since I left. When I came out here earlier, it was to inform you of his loss but the emergency call stopped me. The call was for operating room ten which is the same room that we were operating on your friend in. I found when I came into the room that somehow his heart had begun to beat again on its own. I continued the surgery and we've moved him into the Intensive Care Unit. He is, by no means, and I do mean, no means, out of the woods yet. The next seventy-two hours are the most crucial. I removed every bullet. I was fortunate enough to be able to reach the one in his brain as well We don't know about how bad the brain damage is yet. There certainly has been truama to the brain itself. Right now, its just too early to know anything but we'll allow you to see him for a few minutes if you like."

"Yes," they all said in unison.

Geno had, what seemed, a million tubes coming from his face and arms. Ten machines monoriting ten different vitals. Lights were blinking, beeping or both. Gauze was wrapped around Geno's head. His black face was ashen, looked as if it had seen death.

Monster was wrapped up in his emotions. He was furious and sad. He didn't know who had betrayed him, and his best friend lie still in front of him two inches from the grave and moving all the more closer. He needed Geno alive. Only Geno could tell him who he'd seen, which would mean that he couldn't have been the one to betray the set. Unless, of course, Geno himself got double crossed.

I know it ain't Geno. I can't see Day Day or T.Y. doing this shit either, but I'll find out soon enough, he thought as he patted Geno's hand.

"I'll hit y'all niggas tomorrow," he said to Day Day and T.Y. as they left the room. "Oh, and keep Geno being alive on the hush hush. I don't want anybody knowing." He watched their eyes and searched both faces for the slightest glimmer of guilt. I could swear them niggas is clean, Monster thought. But he knew it was something amiss and that he would figure it out in due time.

Monster drove home smoking a blunt from last night. The smoke was filling the interior of the cabin like a heavy fog, blurring his senses, yet providing him with a clarity of mind. The herb, for Monster, was a stress relief. It was nearly nine o'clock in the evening and the sun was gone. You could see the remnants of it, however, as fading colors in the nighttime sky left their trail across the clouds.

The rain had begun an hour before Monster left the hospital and it remained constant. The consistent pitter patter of the fat drops could either unnerve a man or lend to his gathering of peace. He had left a personal guard outside Geno's room so that there could be no further attempts on his life. That was a major concern.

Somebody's got to die, he knew. Who? was the question. The paranoia behind the weed isn't always a bad side effect. At least, its not on this night, Monster figured. Because he could've sworn-that a car had been behind him ever since he'd stopped at McDonalds earlier. Let's see if I have a tail, he thought.

"Yeah, Wyan Wyan, I'm right behind him. Nah, nigga, not right right behind him. What, you think I'm stupid? I don't want the nigga to see me. Yeah, it's me and Boo Boo. We seen him coming out of Micky D's, but! Hold up, he turning. Yeah, aiight. Soon as he stop, we gonna ice this nigga. Yep, peace," Herbie Luv Bug said as he hung up his cell phone. He turned to Boo Boo, &young nigga who'd recently just shot a girl because he wanted to be funny.

"Ay, Wyan Wyan said to burn this nigga. You ready? Soon as he stop. I don't give a fuck if it's a red light or a gas station, feel me?" Herbie said.

"Oh, no doubt!" Boo Boo quipped happily as he smoked the blunt.

Monster checked his .357 as he rode down the quiet neighborhood street. He knew it was a tail, they tried too hard not to appear to be following him. Niggas is crazy, he thought. I been in this shit for over ten years and these niggas playing.

He parallel parked in front of an unknown house on an unknown street and waited while he smoked his blunt. He saw the tail come down the street with the headlights off. They parked about three houses behind him. There were maybe four cars between them. Monster watched the passenger door open and he slid out the driver side door of his black on black Benz, and duck walked to the rear, stooping behind his car.

In the dead of night he was always an animal victorious.

Boldly he still chiefed on his herb as the nigga who'd just hopped out of the tailing car crept down the street to the side of the Benz, walking right past the crouching Monster. Since he'd been smoking, he couldn't really smell Monster smoking a blunt as he made it past him. He looked into the passenger window but couldn't see throught the double layered ting.

Monster came behind him as Boo Boo raised his pistol at the car's window. "Don't shoot my fucking car," Monster said calmly. The young boy jumped at the sound of his voice, startled that someone was behind him, and turned to face the person speaking. He saw the eyes of a veteran gangster, he saw the face of a goon of the highest degree and his shock and awe were palpable. His eyes went wide, and just before he could raise the gun to his target, he was slammed backward with three slugs from the compact .357.

The gun shots sounded off deafeningly as the powerful bullets ripped holes the size of an orange out of the young man's back after passing through his chest and abdomen. Monster turned to deal with whomever the driver was.

The nigga was running up, aiming, and when Monster tried toshoot him, his gun jammed. "Fuck!" he glowered. he took off and Herbie let off about five shots. Still carrying his gun, he knew he had to do something quick. He knew this young nigga's aim was terrible. Couldn't hit the ground with a rock he dropped. Monster stopped abruptly and pivoted on his lead foot, turned one hundred eighty degrees, and threw his .357 with all of his might. He let out an audible "umph" as he let the pistol fly like the Desert Eagle that it was.

The heavy metal weapon crashed into Herbie Luv Bug's face, knocking out four teeth instantly and spraying the air with a mist of blood. He was asleep before he even hit the ground, head first. When Monster walked up and saw that it was Herbie, he knew that he'd hit pay dirt. "Favor for a favor," he said aloud. "More favors. Favors for everybody."

CHAPTER 18

WELL, WELL, WELL

"Well, well, well," Day Day said, "look what we have here. Look who's decided to wake up."

Day Day, T.Y. and Monster were inside one of Monster's abandoned buildings that they kept around the city for purposes such as this. Herbie Luv Bug opened his eyes and could make out six people. Then his vision shifted and he saw those six people merge and become three. He could see clearly now.

Fuck, he thought, my fuckin' face is on fire, and I'm sitting tied the fuck up in front of these niggers. He spoke as well as he could while his face was as swollen as a bladder. "We didn't kidnap ya girl, dude..." T.Y. cut him off with a swift right hook that blackened his eye. Instantly.

"So, how you know she was gone, asshole? How you know she got kidnapped? Shut the fuck up!" Monster shot as Herbie began to speak. "Where she at?" He asked.

"With Bone Neck... she with Bone."

"No shit, Sherlock, I know that. Where he got her at?"

"He ain't got her nowhere. She with that nigga somewhere."

"What? Ay, this nigga's cuckoo for coacoa puffs. He ain't

making no sense. Fuck it, kill him," Day Day said.

"Yeah, you right, Day Day. But we gonna have some fun with this nigga first. His boss man should be calling soon. Hand me that rubbing alcohol, T.Y." Once he passed him a large gallon sized jug of alcohol, Monster then took out a rusted box cutter and sliced away Herbie Luv Bug's clothes.

"What's up, noodle nuts?" Day Day joked at Herbie's little dick.

"Herbie No LUV Bug!" T.Y. said and they all laughed heartily. Except Herbie. He didn't laugh at all. For him, nothing was funny. Understandable.

Monster sliced across Herbie's forehead with the razor. The pain was sharp, like the blade, causing him to wince and then, just as suddenly, he began to scream. When he opened his mouth and began that blood curdling scream Monster grabbed his lower lip fiercely and with the razor, sawed it off. He was using barbarian tactics.

The blood was flowing profusely. Day Day: filled up a water gun that he had bought with the rubbing alcohol and some bleach.

"What's all this shit for?" T.Y. asked over Herbie's simpering cries.

"Monster has perfected the craft of torture," Day Day replied, nodding in the direction of the scene in front of him, imploring T.Y. to watch what was about to unfold. "Watch and learn," he finished.

Monster was carving away at Herbie Luv Bug. He was going at him like a holiday ham. His chest, his thighs, ankles, knees, everywhere he was receiving gashes, but not large enough to bleed him out quickly. The slices were just past the flesh.

Herbie was covered in blood, sweat, and tears.

"Gimmie the pellet gun," Monster said. He began peppering Herbie's nuts with pellets.

"Oww!" he screamed as T.Y. screwed up his face in sympathetic pain. Any man could tell that what Herbie was going through was likely as bad as it got.

"Shit! Monster ill as fuck!" he exclaimed. "But, the fuck is the alcohol and bleach for?" he asked Day Day as Monster was still having target practice.

"That's the clincher," Day Day said as he took the pellet gun from Monster and began to have his own fun. Suddenly Herbie's phone rang.

"There we go," Monster declared reading Wyan Wyan's name on the caller I.D. "Been waiting on this."

"Hello? Herbie?" Wyan said into the phone.

Monster put on his best secretary voice, "Hello. Kidnapper and murder hotline. Torture a plus but not required, how may we assist you today?" Monster said laughing.

"Herbie, what the fuck? Quit playing, man! I been waiting on you to call me back for bout two hours now. You get that bitch nigga or what?" Wyan Wyan screamed into the phone.

"He ain't get shit but fucked up! 01' hoe ass nigga," Monster said back in reply.

"The fuck?" Wyan said confused.

"Yup, nigga. Now the question is, do you got my bitch? I got your number one nigga. Oh, don't think I want to deal, but. 'Cause I'm killing this pussy. That's my word. And I'mma do it with you on the phone. Wouldn't want any misunderstandings you know?" Monster nodded and Day Day handed T.Y. the super soaker and told him what to do. The smile that grew on

T.Y.'s face was fiendish.

On cue, T.Y. let loose the water canon. The bleach and alcohol concoction reacted viciously to the multiple cuts and bloody wounds that Herbie had obtained that night. The water canon let loose its payload all over Herbie Luv Bug and he suffered the most severe pain that he could ever imagine existed.

He let loose a violent, blood wrenching scream that authored the tale of how devastating was the sensation that he was experiencing.

"Nigga, don't you know if you kill Herbie, I'mma murk yo' bitch?" Wyan said so desperately you could smell it. He was fishing for a way to save his own best friend.

"Nigga, that's just gonna be considered a casualty of war," Monster said grimly. He really didn't want it to be like that but he had to be what he was. A Monster. ,Can't let love get in the way of war. War was brutal and during that time, one had to be that way as well. "Say goodbye to Herbie Luv Bug, Wyan Wyan," Monster said as he, T.Y. and Day Day aimed their guns at him.

They all let fire their pistol,, each emptying an entire magazine into the body of the man that they had successfully kidnapped and tortured nearly to death. "That was for my nigga, Geno. Bitch, you next. Tell Bone Neck that I'll see him when I see him."

'CLICK.'

CHAPTER 19

ALL'S FAIR IN LOVE & WAR

In the grim of the night, Day Day and T.Y. sat with Monster inside of his condo talking. Monster spoke next, "So, I gotta figure out which one of y'all two niggas is the turncoat."

"Why just us?" T.Y. said.

"Monster is sure already that it wasn't Geno, just like I know it ain't him. I decided that and figured it out on my own, and so did he," Day Day told T.Y.

"Right," Monster said snacking on a piece of fried chicken from Popeyes. "For the first time in my life, I'm unsure of shit. But I can guaren-damn-tee that I'mma find out who it is. Any confessions? Die with honor and tell me now!" Monster said grimacing. He searched their eyes time and again for the tell tale signs but came up empty. "I swear its like both of y'all niggas is clean. I ain't gonna get stupid and start treating y'all no different than before," Monster said with a sigh.

"Here," he said, giving them each a duffel bag. "A weeks

pay, plus tonight's bonus. T.Y., you got anything?" Monster asked.

"Nope. Look closer though. That's all I can say, Monster. Look closer," T.Y. responded. I really want to tell him, he thought to himself, but he won't believe me. I have to help him find out, he decided evenly.

"Alright, y'all, holla. Peace," Monster said as he escorted them to the door.

"Poison," T.Y. said before leaving. "One's poison is another man's treasure," he said as he left Monster looking dumbfounded.

"Yo, what's up?" Monster said, answering his iphone.

"You fucked up, nigga!" Bone Neck spat from his end.

"Bitch, what you want, bum ass nigga? Oh, your broke ass need five millie, don't you? Damn, you broke, Bone Neck. How you get the name 'Bone Neck' anyway? Yeah, we gonna have to change that shit to Broke Neck, 'cause your bitch ass broke as fuck. Ay, how that sound? You think it'll work?" Monster chuckled as he amused himself and taunted Bone Neck.

"Fuck you, Monster. You want your bitch back, right? Come off them pesos, then bull," he responded.

"You know, I'm starting to have second thoughts, Mr. Broke Neck. Since I murked Herbie last night, then y'all prolly killed her already, so I'mma pass on this one. Maybe next time, okay?" 'CLICK.' Monster hung up with conviction in his heart and tears in his eyes. He hoped he was wrong but this was the game that he played. The game he had to play. Carefree. Cold muthafucka. That's who you had to be in war. Today was Shock and Awe. Today anybody would die.

"Hello? Day Day, how it's looking? Everybody ready?

Alright, then tell them niggas to move out. Drop the whips off and lay low for about two days. Nobody should know who did it, but if I got a leak then they might," Monster said to Day Day over his celly. "I don't want young T.Y. with them niggas. They go alone. Time to prove loyalty!"

Monster had brought ten small Hondas, untraceable, scrubbed completely, and had them delivered to his strip where his young ruthless niggas live. On 7th Street. Each one had three choppers fully loaded with no additional clips. The plan was for his young niggas to go four in each whip and three would shoot up 5th Street's mainline. No children. If a child got hit and died, Monster would pick the block leader out and they would find out who had done it and kill them. If they couldn't find them, Monster would kill the block leader. Ten cars, thirty choppers, nine hundred and sixty rounds. Murder.

"Alright, Monster, just turn on the news in about twenty or thirty minutes. Holla."

"Peace," Monster said as he hung up from Day Day. He lit up a burner and opened a bottle of Remy Martin XO. He sat and began to contemplate everything that had been going on. he flicked on the t.v. and waited for the news break that was sure to come. Monster began to drift away into his thoughts. Or sleep. Or both.

Who's betraying me? It can't be Geno. Day Day has been with me too long. Could he? Then there's. Young T.Y. I do everything for that young nigga. I don't see no reason for this shit. But is there always a reason for treachery? T.Y. knows something but he don't want to say. Or won't say. Or can't say. I'm pretty sure that it's not him. Why would he bring it up if it was? To threw me off? Then, for that matter, I know it ain't Day

Day either. This is too much stress. Okay, okay, Monster. Think about it. The clues. The clues. Geno said, "What are you doing here?" Who was he surprised to see? Not Bone Neck 'cause we knew he was a back stabber. He would have called out to Day Day or to T.Y. What am I missing? Poison? What does that mean? There's something about the apartment. When I came home that day. Something's not right. A noise. What noise? It was...

His dream-like state of thought was interrupted by the TV and the news anchor speaking excitedly yet somber. "Yes, here on Philadelphia's south side, gunfire erupted from what is being called an army of Hondas. Powerful assault rifles have destroyed at least eight homes. The body count is up to seventeen now...

Instantly, Monster Week flashed through his mind. He smiled at the idea.

"...We are live here and it is chaos. Absolute chaos and havoc on the street. Police cruisers are all over the city pulling over Hondas. We haven't been informed of any suspects being apprehended as of yet. It appears that the assailants tossed out all of their weapons which, as we have seen, are fully automatic AK47 style assault rifles. Now, this is either very smart or very dumb. It would be silly because if these hoodlums left their fingerprints, then our excellent police force should be hot on their tails. It would however be very intelligent if there are no fingerprints or dna because no matter how many Hondas the cops find and pull over, none will have the firearms necessary to link them to such a grisly murder scene. Mass bloodshed, people. Mass.

"We have an eyewitness here who claims to have seen the

entire thing. His name is uh, Apple Cider? Mr. Cider, please give us your account."

Apple Cider. was a crackhead. Monster began to smile because he knew that this would be good.

Then he spoke, "My account? Naw man, I don't go to no banks. It's a violation of my parole. I thought you wanted to know what I seen? Oh, okay, then, yeah, yeah, five cars came from up by Omar house and then like five mo' came from down by Gene's crib. Gene gotta cute little sister, though, anyway, they started bustin' and niggas oops! I can't say that, huh? Oh fuck it, niggas ran and I dipped out too. Shiiiit, I ain't getting popped for nobody. Ohhh, there go Omar right there. Ay, Omar! You got some butter?" Apple Cider ran to Omar to score some dope more than likely. The interview was a disaster. The newscaster was probably going to either get fired or severely reprimanded for that one.

"There we have it, folks, ten cars disintegrated these fallen homes and have killed at least, what is it now? Wow! Twenty people have now lost their lives, folks. Stay tuned for more..." Monster hit the mute button on the remote. He had made the first and second move.

The only way these suckas can keep up is 'cause they got Bone Neck with them. He kind of smart because I taught him how to be, Monster thought. His cell phone rang.

"What it is?" he answered.

"Crazy shit on the news," Day Day said.

"I know, I just saw it. What's this world coming to? Whoever did that was some animals, huh?" Monster replied. then said, "Anybody get caught?"

"The news anchor said, 'no,' " Day Day responded in code.

"Peace."

"Yup, I'll holla," Day Day responded.

They both knew that it was a possibility that the phone he'd called Monster on could be tapped. Then his real phone rang. He was smarter than your average. One phone that he knew was likely on tap, he kept and used, just to put out misinformation and to provide alibis to himself and his crew, and one in which he really did his thing on. And even that was an untraceable burner phone.

"Holla," he answered.

"E! E! Help me!" called Fay's crying voice on the other end.

"Fay!" Monster shouted hysterically. "Where you at, girl? I'mma come and..."

"Nope. You ain't doing shit but giving me my muhfuckin money, nigga!" Bone Neck broke in through the receiver. "I need seven mil now, nigga. You got I'mma be nice... you got two days. I'mma hit you back in two days with the drop off information. If one more nigga die, I mean if a nigga even cut himself shaving, I'mma kill this slut. Oh, don't make me rape her while you listen, nigga. You niggas done pissed me off. Forty-eight hours or I'm torturing shit!" 'CLICK.'

Monster didn't want to be responsible for Fay's death. Not over some money that he could easily replace. But it might be a set up. And it most likely was. Monster slumped back into his couch, sipping his Remy and blazing a cigarello. He was soon fast asleep. Fast.

"That muhthafucka murked twenty-two niggas. Six still might not make it! Bone Neck, what the fuck?" Wyan Wyan screamed.

"Ay, bull, I told you the nigga is dangerous. I explained all of the possible repercussions before we got into this shit. I told you either you, me or Herb might die. Plus more. I told you that he would find ya momma if you piss him off enough. Plus more. And that Geno shit did it. Good thing he dead. Don't want that nigga telling about our little parner, you feel me?" Bone Neck said to Wyan who was still fuming.

"Man, Herbie might still be alive. We ain't found his body yet. The nigga might of bluffed us, bull," Wyan Wyan maintained hopefully.

"Is Geno still alive?" Bone Neck asked. "No," he answered his own question. "Then neither the fuck is Herbie fucking Luv Bug," he said with conviction. ""Monster don't play no games like that, nigga. I upped our pay to seven mil, though. Don't worry, ain't nobody else gonna wind up dead. he don't want his little bitch dead."

"Oh, so he don't know?"

"Of course he don't know, nigga! He wouldn't pay if he did," Bone Neck finished.

"Oh, this gonna be good. Real good."

"What time is it?" Monster asked Day Day as he and T.Y. walked into Monster's home.

"It's time to get up, young bull," Day Day declared as he glanced at the empty fifth of Remy. "You fucked up, huh? Well, it shouldn't matter, 'cause we gotta take care of this business, my nigga. Let's move," Day Day instructed.

"Day Day, man, they want seven mil for Fay. Faaaaayy!" Monster cried out drunkenly.

"Man, fuck that bitch, nigga! Let's handle this shit for Geno," T.Y. spat with anger.

"What you say, nigga? Watch your mouth, T.Y. 'That's my

future wife, you talking 'bout nigga," Monster said hiccupping most of his words and slurring the rest.

"Monster, you mad bugging," T.Y. said shaking his head.

"Monster, you need to sober up, bull. Take another nap and then shower. We going to get something to eat. We gonna move this shit up about four hours," Day Day said, taking control.

"They say Fay gon' get killed if we murk another one of their niggas," Monster managed before finally passing out.

"This ain't one of their niggas. And like T.Y. said, 'fuck that bitch," Day Day said. But Monster was already snoring lightly.

"Ruthless," T.Y. said high as a motherfucker, "I"m ruthless as fuck. Watch. I got something for this nigga tonight. Don't get mad at me, y'all. I hate cops. Monster, you aiight?" T.Y. asked.

"Yeah, I'm straight, young bull we almost there. I heard his wife mad young and shit. Like twenty-five or something. And she fine as wine," Monster responded.

"Well, she gonna have to go. We can't have no witnesses. This serious right here," Day Day said. "T.Y., how you find out where this nigga live at?" Monster asked. "I been trying for years to find out. Niggas be scared to follow him."

"I told you, Monster. I'm one with the streets. Like a Jedi and shit. And, yeah, his wife is cold. I seen her. We gonna get more acquainted tonight," T.Y. said with a chuckle. "Pull up right here," he said to Day Day.

It was a warm evening at around seventy-five degrees and nearly midnight. They could see lights on inside the house and decided that the best idea would be to knock. he didn't expect this bit of company and when he came to the door, the alarm would be off. Also, they knew he would open the door all the way if he couldn't see anyone from the peephole. He was too cocky to suspect foul play on him. Oh No! Not him. He thought he was too tough.

Monster and Day Day stooped on one side of the door and T.Y. was on the other. He knocked hard. They all had silenced .22 caliber hand guns. Assassins weapons.

"Who is it?" the loud voice bellowed from the other side of the heavy wood door. "Dammit! Fucking Nigger knockers!" he yelled when he got no response. Snoop yanked the door open ferociously. Once the light from the interior of the home spilled out onto the fornt porch, Monster jerked open the screen door as he stood up to his full height, and put the pistol to Snoop's face. Day Day came in behind and T.Y. was last.

""Who is it, hun?" asked a woman's voice from the stairway in the hall.

"Tell her to come and see," Monster whispered.

"Uh, come down and see, hun," he suggested in a semi-spry voice.

T.Y. waited out of sight by the stairs as she descended gracefully to the bottom landing. When she touched the landing,, he grabbed her an put a hand over her mouth. Her eyes went wide with shock and initially, she thrashed about, not understanding the full gravity of the situation.

"Scream and I'll put your brains all over your husband," T.Y. said to her with violence emanating from his tone. "Understood?" he asked, seeking confirmation. She nodded her reply as tears welled in her eyes. Day Day's eyes grew wide at the sight of the young white girl with full breasts and a voluptuous ass. Not at her body, though. But at recognition.

"Yo, Monster, you know who she is, don't you?" Day Day called over to him, grabbing his attention.

"No shit," Monster said surprised as he looked at Snoop with evil intent. "So, this is your wife, huh? Fucking shit head, I should've known," Monster said. They tied up the couple and gagged them after stripping them down to their birthday suits. Monster then told T.Y. the story of the white girl in the chair.

"Yeah, T.Y., her name is Chae. Five years or so ago, she came through the hood and left with like three of my young block leaders. you know, niggas was expecting the G.P. edition, you feel me? Check it out, though. She let all three of my young'uns run a train on her like rail road tracks, right? So two hours later, all three are in jail for rape. They all ended up copping pleas because they were afraid to go to trail against a white girl. I told them that I had it covered, but they couldn't hold up. It was too heavy.

"Since she was married to a cop whose name they wouldn't release, my young niggas got ten years each. They can't appeal their case either. Then I got a letter after they got sentenced that said, 'If we can't get you for drugs and murder, we'll get you for rape. Nigger!' So I knew it was a set up. And look who we got here," Monster finished.

He then took off Snoop's gag and talked to him. "You fucked with me for too long, Snoop. I'm sick of your shit," Monster exclaimed.

"You're not going to get away with kidnapping a cop and his wife! I'll testify in court. Or I'll kill you first. You fucking maggot!" Snoop spat out. His attempt at bluster and threat was pathetic.

Monster merely laughed at the fact that Snoop actually thought that he would live to testify or to get any kind of revenge. "Do what y'all do," he said to Day Day and T.Y. "I'm going to watch t.v. You got cable? No? How about maybe satellite? Oh okay, you's a satellite guy, huh? See you soon, bye bye then," Monster joked at Snoop as he left to go watch TV

Day Day gagged Snoop again and then ungagged and untied Chae. "You like to accuse muhfuckas of rape on some false shit, huh?" T.Y. said. Snoop's eyes got wide as T.Y. threw Chae onto the bed and pulled out his dick. "Suck it, bitch!" he screamed. And she did. "Look at this shit," T.Y. declared. "She likes this shit. I'll be damned!"

Chae pushed T.Y. onto the bed and took over like a pro. She was sucking his soul out. She pulled down T.Y.'s pants all the way and straddled him. Snoop was furious. He thrased against the ties and gurgled angry sounds in his throat but that was the extent of what he could do in his present state of indisposal.

Day Day hopped onto the bed and he and T.Y. had their way with Chae. And she enjoyed every minute of it. Just as she had five years before. Slut, Day Day thought.

Snoop phone began to ring and Monster merely stared at it until the answering machine picked up.

"Ay, Snoop, answer the damn phone, muhfucka! Probably fucking your no-good wife, huh? Naw, I'm fucking with you, but look, I gave Monster two days to get his shit tight. I'mma call you when it get ready to go down, so you can slide through and fuck him up. You know, ambush the nigger or something. Just in case I don't talk to you by then, I'm setting it up on Third Street in the alley. Ten o'clock at night in two days, alright? That's the day after tomorrow in case you stupid... ha ha... see, I'm fucking with you again. Let's get this paper," Wyan Wyan's voice clicked off as he hung up the phone.

"What the fuck?" Monster stared incredulously at the phone.

He couldn't believe how dumb these niggas could be. First of all, who still has an answering machine? he thought. And second, who the fuck leaves a shithead ass message like that on one? Monster walked into the bedroom and saw what looked like a porno being shot.

T.Y. had his phone out recording it as she got the train ran on her. He was dancing and flexing for the camera. He stupid, Monster chuckled to himself before speaking. "Change of plans, y'all," Monster began. "Nobody dies tonight." Then he smiled as Day Day and T.Y. watched him join in the action.

CHAPTER 20

SECRETS FROM THE GRAVE

After placing Chae and Snoop in the back of Monster's Navigator, they transported them to his condo in OverBrook. He explained everything to Day Day and T.Y. on the way there. They could only have fun with Chae for one more day and they could continue to torture Snoop.

This was going to be good, Monster knew. Good thing that he hadn't killed them before the call. They slept at Monster's crib that night until about two in the afternoon. Chae and Snoop were forced to sleep in the chairs that they were tied to. Chae, however, was freed at various intervals throughout the night to perform sexual favors which she didn't seem to mind. She had the perpetual thought that maybe if she were good then she would be allowed to live. Freak bitch, Monster thought to himself.

"Tomorrow night this shit goes down, so be ready, y'all," Monster said as T.Y. and Day Day were leaving the house.

"Take today off and chill. You've earned it. Oh, try not to kill any Fifth Street niggas," he called out before the door shut.

He decided to sit with Snoop for a while. he removed his gag in order to have a two way conversation with him. "Why you been chasing me for so long? What I do to you?"

"You aren't shit, Moore. You eat, sleep, and breathe shit. Always murdering people and selling drugs. Always in shit. I'm a cop. It's my job to be after your ass!" Snoop quipped.

"Aww don't play that 'I'm just doing my job bit with me, Snoop. That's some cold bullshit. Y'all cops do murder. Y'all bang dope and weed. Plus y'all racists and y'all set niggas up so they get booked. Just look at how you and wifey did my homeboys a few years back. What makes you better than me?" Monster asked.

I get paid for it." Snoop said with a smirk.

"Hmm... so do I." Monster shot back. "Except I make millions, you don't' That's ,,why you can't stand me. huh? Yeah. I just figured it all out. You do what I do. I'm just better at it. And you hate me for it."

"Fuck you, Moore. You wait until I get free." Snoop said.

"News flash. dickface. you getting free is like waiting for the sun to rise at night. Ain't gunna happen. You die. Ya bitch dies. If you had a dog. that muthafucka would die. too. 'You don't have a dog do you? Anyway. you had something to do with Geno getting shot." Monster pressed.

"No-no. I didn't. What made you figure that?"

"Somebody left a special message on your answering machine last night. You better stop associating with shit. Your colle ues may find you, ya think? Don't worry. tnough- I took the tape and unplugged the answering machine and phone since you didn't have the common sense to deal with niggas that know better than to leave a message like that. They wouldn't know. You should thank me. Really. I looked out for you on this one. You'll die with a good name." Monster said Smugly.

"No. you don't understand. It wasn't just me. It was... it..."

"Who?!" Monster could feel himself getting close to the truth. "Who. snoop?"

"Ahh. I have something you want. 'eh? Well. 1 want my freedom..." he began to look pleased with himself as Monster cut him off With the a swift gun butt across the face. "That won'y do it. Moore. I want to be let go." he said spitting out blood and a tooth or two.

Monster raged him. "Fuck you Snoop. I don't negotiate with terrorist. You're a terrorist to my organization. You die."

Monster was tired. Exhausted. Sick of the game. He had well over twenty million in his savings and at least fifty bricks of soda and dog food just sitting, waiting on him to make a move or two. He could dump all of it wholesale and sell all of his homes and businesses. It could all get him close to another twenty million or so. That ain't bad. Leaving the game with a cool forty. But I got other people to feed. And I got my pact. Something gots to shake. Soon, Monster thought solemnly. he decided to pass money out to all of his young niggas today. All the ones who pulled that caper for him the other day. He left and got into his car.

"Young Toby! What's popping my young block buster?" Monster spoke to his newest block leader as he pulled up on 7th Street. This one had a mouth full of jewels and was eager, ambitious, and loyal. Reminded Monster of Young T.Y. It's a never ending cycle, he concluded. "Y'all niggas had some fun?"

"Hell yeah, Monster!-Anything for the set. You know how we get down. We need, you feed."

"Yeah, I know," Monster said. "you know what to do with the funds. Split it up with them niggas that went with you. Take this shit up in the building. Don't let nobody see it, Alright?" Monster said, handing Toby a duffle bag that he could barely carry.

"Damn, old head, how much in this muhfucka?"

"Toby, get your dirty ass out of here, ha ha. Six hundred stacks, nigga. That's fifteen bands each. Handle that. Eat up."

"Damn, thug, I knew you was paid but Goddamn! You know I'mma take care of this shit for you. I'm loyal, Monster... I'mma show you!" Toby said enthusiastically.

"I know, Toby. Get at me. Peace."

"Peace," Toby responded waddling off with more cash than he had ever seen in his entire life.

Monster knew the money would get dished out evenly. Niggas were scared to steal from Monster. They knew he killed whenever, however. He began to laugh to himself at the thought of Snoop and his wife tied up and chained in his basement. there would be all kinds of new whips riding around the hood from that bonus he just gave out. Gotta give back. Otherwise the hood gon' take back, he thought respectfully.

For the majority of the day, Monster decided to just cruise around and smoke by himself. That's just what he did until he found himself in the hospital's parking lot. Somwhere inside, he missed Geno. It was time to check on his friend and see about his progress. To see if his boy was okay.

Briefly, he spoke with the nurse who'd told him that Geno was out of the woods. He was in and out of consciousness but had not spoken a word yet. Monster looked over his fallen soldier and anger filled him. Tears lined his eyes as he searched his friend's face for a sign of life. There were none. Upset, he chose to sit and calm down.

He held Geno's hand and began to speak. "Geno. Man, I'm sorry. Now that all this happened, I know it ain't worth it. Man, I'm tired, bull. I'm exhausted. Close to eleven years we been in. I wanna retire. Fuck the pact, Geno. Let's pick up and go when you get better, bull. Me, you, Day Day, and even little T.Y. crazy ass can roll. That's my nigga. I got about four cribs outside the country. In some nice spots, homie. We can chill and just enjoy life, you dig? You gotta wake up, Geno, 'cause a nigga need you. Doctors say you gon live but you might be fucked up. they say your head fucked up, Geno. They don't know if you're coming out of unconsciousness or if your body is just doing it's own thing. I need you to..." Monster stopped when he felt Geno's hand tighten the tiniest bit. He looked and Geno's eyes fluttered open. Monster stood up and looked at his friend.

"What's up, young bull? Can you talk?"

"B-b," was all he seemed to be able to mutter. A muffled and seemingly indistinguishable sound. "'B--Bone," Geno stammered out.

"I know, Geno. It's cool. Don't talk, man. I know it was Bone Neck," Monster said.

"B-Bone Neck want Fay want money. Shot Fay, and Bone me," he finished in a confusion of jumble that didn't make much sense to Monster.

Monster was clueless and did not understand one bit of what Geno was trying to say. The nurse ran in and ushered Monster out so that they could run tests on Geno while he was still conscious.

Monster sat in the waiting room until midnight. the doctor finally came after hours and hours of waiting. "Mr. Moore Geno is asleep. We've sedated him and are running neurological tests to see about brain damage," the doctor said as he continued, "You should go home and get some sleep. Your friend seems to have some speech pattern issues from the brain trauma. He's speaking slightly out of sync but is expected to return to normal conversation after a while. But then again we won't know for sure until we run some more tests and allow his body to heal. That's the waiting game. To see what his body does on its own. There are some problems and recoveries that we in the medical field can never predict or explain. My vote to you is pray."

Monster had some questions, though. "What do you mean, 'he speaks out of sync?' "

"Well, when asked his name, he responded with his last name first and then his first name, in reverse order. His speech is impaired and out of order but as I said, he should recover."

"But does he make sense? I mean, does he understand what he's trying to say?"

"I'd like to think he does. You have to piece together what he says. Maybe substitute a word or two and change the order but if you do that, you should get a perfect meaning out of his context. Why? Did he speak to you?"

"No, no, nothing like that, Doctor. I'm tired. I'll check on him in a day or so. Thanks."

"No problem, Mr. Moore. Take it easy."

"Sure thing, Doc. Sure thing."

Monster rode home in his Tahoe and let his mind wander. Things were trying to piece together but he was still missing something. He just couldn't put his finger on what the puzzle was missing.

A noise when I came home? What noise? Poison? Geno said, "Bone Neck want Fay want money. Shot Fay. And Bone Neck me." What is it that he meant? Herbie Luv Bug said they didn't kidnap her. So what the fuck? The doctor said that Geno was talking in riddles or something. "Shot fay and Bone Neck me." Oh shit! Bone Neck shot Fay and Geno. They're trying to get money from me and she's dead? But there are still missing pieces. They'll come but now, for the time being, I gotta assume that she is dead. Damn.

Monster put in Geno's favorite oldies by Bel Biv Devo. His favorite song was "Poison." He sang along, off key. "It's driving me out of my mind. That's why its hard for me to find. Can't get it outta my head. Miss her, kiss her, love her, that girl is POOOiisssoon!"

Monster had a revelation. The biggest revelation. "Fucking fuck!" Monster screamed aloud as he headed back to his spot in Overbrook. He had figured it out. How could he let it slip past him. Oh, there will be hell to pay, thought Monster angrily. Hell. To. Pay.

CHAPTER 21

REVELATIONS

Monster was pissed. He ran into the house and T.Y. and Day Day were on the couch. "What's up, Monster?" T.Y. called. "I moved them to the bedroom. I had to have some fun, you know?"

Monster pulled off his shirt and reached into his safe spot in the cabinet for his .22 with the silencer on it. Day Day and T.Y. watched in silent approximation. "O--okay. Monster's off his rocker," Day Day said. Monster rushed into the bedroom and they followed.

Chae was asleep and Snoop sat with his eyes open but he was bleeding very heavily. It looked as if T.Y. and Day Day had thrown him in a meat grater. Monster could smell isopropyl alcohol. He saw the water gun on the table and looked at Day Day who shrugged his shoulders and pointed at the smiling T.Y.

"Alright, bitch, you gonna play games?!" Monster yelled at the struggling Snoop. Chae jostled awake and Monster yanked off her gag. He pulled Nookie Monster out and jammed him as hard as he could into her mouth and she gagged. Monster banged her mouth so hard that she began to cry. "you gonna tell me Snoop? Or do I keep going? You gonna fucking tell me? No? Oh well, I like this better," Monster resounded.

Day Day and T.Y. watched in awe. Monster pulled out and finished on her face. He then grabbed his banger and shot her four times in the chest. Her blood exploded onto the bed, walls, and carpet in a wash of crimson tide. Snoop was wailing as loud as a gagged man could.

"It's all your fucking fault. You chose to keep shit from me. She could've died with you. Now you die alone. Tonight!" Monster affirmed. Monster shot him once in the thigh. He lit the stove and pawed in hot honey to cauterize the wound.

"What's going on?" Day Day asked as he helped Monster clean up all the blood.

"We're taking the body and all the shit with blood on it and burning it," he replied.

"Nigga, don't act crazy. You know what I mean," Day Day scolded. "I'll tell you and T.Y. when we finish."

They took the body out about ten miles and lit it and all of the other evidence afire. A cop's dead wife would alert the city so they burned her so that she couldn't be identified. They also knocked out all of her teeth to avoid any dental records being used. He told T.Y. and Day Day the whole thing on the way home.

"So, after I put in the song and I sang the lyrics, I had a very important revelation. When I came home, I remembered a distinct noise but I wrote it off so routinely. I was so used to disarming my security system, that it hadn't dawned on me that

I should have not had to do that. The security system never went off during the 'break-in.' Which means, it was set before they left. On top of that, the door was locked when I got there. Next is what Herbie said. 'We didn't kidnap ya girl, dud.' Remember, after we asked him where she was at? He said that she was with Bone Neck. Day Day said, 'No shit, we know that. Where he got her at?' And the nigga said that she was with that nigga somewhere. We thought he was talking stupid. But he was saying that he ain't make her go nowhere. She was with that nigga on her own. Get it? No? Aiight, pin this, damn let me tap the blunt, nigga... you a hoover! Anyway, peep game, remember Geno was suprised at who was at his crib when he got shot? He would have called out to either one of you for help, right? Look it gets better...

"Remember the doctor told me that his speech is fucked up. So, you gotta figure it out. Geno said 'Bone Neck want Fay want money.' He was saying that Bone Neck and Fay wanted money. then he said shot fay and Bone Neck me.' I had that fucked up for a second. The doctor said he was popped with two guns, right? So Geno killed one nigga all his bullets were not found in Geno. So what he was saying was, and it's easy now, Bone and Fay shot me. I was thinking she was dead, then I remembered that I talked to her after that. Also, who told me about Bone Neck flipping? Fay! They both flipped together. Bone is probably fucking her.

And that song tipped me off, T.Y... 'Poison.' " Monster finished proudly. "But you already knew, huh? Why you ain't tell me?"

"Naw, I ain't know. The streets was saying it was me or Day Day but me and him was always together. They then said it was

Geno. But we all knew that was impossible. I just figured that it was Fay. I ain't want to say nothing 'cause niggas act up over their hoes, ya dig? But you pulled it off Sherlock Holmes!" T.Y. said as they all shared in a laugh.

"Now, let's get some sleep, y'all. Niggas got a lotta work ahead of us. When we pull up, we go in and sleep. When we wake up, we get shit started. It's already four thirty in the morning. We got till ten o'clock p.m. for the first part of the plan."

At sundown, Day Day left the condo after a few hours of sleep to set up. He would wait from eight o'clock on, until the meeting in the alley commenced. He was setting up in a window with a high powered fully automatic sniper rifle. Equipped with night scope and silencer. At roughly nine fifteen, T.Y. and Monster placed Snoop's naked ass in the alley. Gagged and chained with a walkie talkie duct taped to him. They were looking through night vision goggles when the phone rang. They knew that it would be Wyan telling Monster to meet him at the drop point. Of course he had no idea that they already knew where the spot was and would already be ready.

Monster answered smugly. "Happy kidnappers and murderers hotline. How may I direct your call?"

They all laughed crazily. It didn't help that they were blunted. T.Y. said, "Man, I'm high as bird tittles!" and they all broke out into raucous laughter again. It was as if they had forgotten that Wyan was on the phone. And he was fuming.

"You gonna quit playing games with me, nigga. What you gonna do, shoot or dribble?"

"Alright, I got the money, broke ass nigga." More laughter. "Where you want me to meet you at so you can get un-broke?"

"Yeah, Alright, funny ass nigga. Meet me in the alley on Third, nigga. You got thirty minutes!" Wyan Wyan hung up, not knowing that Monster was already waiting on him.

Five minutes later, a black sedan pulled in with it's headlamps turned off. This about to be fun, Monster thought solemnly.

Day Day was posted with a premier Heckler and Koch fully automatic sniper rifle, and he was trigger happy. The passenger door opened just before the drivers side door. It was neither Wyan or Bone Neck. Just two regular niggas.

"BOOOO!" Monster booed them like a bad movie. ""Who is these medium ass niggas? Where the starting cast at?" he whispered. The two men noticed the naked Snoop and summoned back to their car. The rear doors opened and out stepped Wyan Wyan and Bone Neck. Everybody was brandishing a gun.

"Pea shooters," Day Day chuckled. Monster buzzed the walkie talkie.

Approaching cautiously, Bone Neck grabbed the walkie talkie from the tape and listened. he nearly dropped it when it crackled to life and he heard Monster speak.

"Don't move a fucking inch. Bone, I got Day Day with me and he got something real big. Shit look real crazy and it shoot like real fast. And I know you think it's mad dark and we up like five stories or more, but check dig, young bull, this nigga gotta night scope, oh this bitch is Monster finished, toying with them.

Bone, Wyan, and the two off brands they brought stood around in a circle enclosed around the struggling Snoop. There was absolutely no light in the alley, if not for the full yellow of the Benz's parking lights.

Bone Neck began, "Monster, you know who you fucking with?"

Monster, feeling cynical, had to respond, "A gun to your head and that's all you can come up with? I found your dude here at his crib. I know he was helping you. I've had my fun with him, as you can imagine. I won't give you a penny for Fay." He played the game. "I'm in favor of the United States Government on this one. I will not negotiate with terrorists." They began to laugh. "Go ahead, see what Snoop has to say. Sure does seem important, don't it, Bone?"

"What should we do?" Wyan whispered to Bone Neck.

"Shit, what can we do?" Take the nigga's gag off. We fucked, you dig? If their serious, anyway," Bone Neck affirmed.

"They sure fucked him up good, though," Wyan Wyan said, unraveling the tape from Snoop's mouth and face.

Just as the tape was coming to an end, Day Day fired a single round. It was a quiet night. From fifteen stories high, the men on the ground could neither hear the clasp of the round firing nor see a muzzle flash, all for the suppression of the top tier silencer.

Just as Snoop was uttering his first real word, there was a sound that was like a cantaloupe hitting the ground at a thousand miles an hour. And a split second after the realization that it sounded like that, was the realization that it was as if it had exploded right in front of them. It was Snoop's head. His melon juices were everywhere and his brain matter splattered the four men surrounding him. Once it had settled in what had happened, all four broke out in a nervous run. Day Day fired well placed rounds. Twenty of them. Intently sending bullets ricocheting off the pavement and garbage bins. they all stopped immediately... knowing shit was real.

Day Day reloaded. "I said don't move," Monster called over the speaker. "Y'all niggas still screaming that red rum, till that lead smack ya back and make ya legs numb." Monster rapped as Day Day pumped ten rounds into the body of one of the regular niggas. Every bullet was in him before he had the chance to hit the ground.

They all started to flinch again and Monster warned them, "Ah, ah, ahhh," he said as Day Day finished the clip off in the other much average nigga. A rat ran across Wyan's foot and a foot later, it exploded as one of the large rifle shells splattered it.

"Look, Wyan crying," T.Y. said, looking through the goggles. Day Day reloaded again. Getting into a groove.

Bone Neck went to scratch his head and Day Day put a bullet four inches from his foot. All that Bone Neck could do was grasp nervously.

"Dont Fucking. Move," Monster reiterated. "That's your problem now, Bone Neck. You don't know how to follow rules." Day Day released a whole clip into Wyan Wyan's sedan. he flattened the tires and totally disabled the car. "Not going anywhere for a while? Grab a Snickers," Monster joked over the mic.

Day Day let off random shots as close as he could get without hitting them as they tried hard to stand still. After they had their fun, Day Day began to place the weapon on a mount and set it computer to automatic. The weapon would fire one, two, or three shots on its own every two minutes from a 50 round magazine in the general area that Day Day would program into it.

The clique left the apartment leaving Wyan Wyan and Bone Neck to stew over what was happening. They stayed in the alley for three hours, thinking that they couldn't move. And when they left, it was on foot.

CHAPTER 22

FALL OF AN EMPIRE

Monster had sold all of his possessions and gotten rid of all his work over the course of the past week, and he was ready. He had decided to give up the game and retire with more money than he could count. He needed an accountant for his accountant, he was so paid. All the paper was transferred to offshore accounts that were untraceable and untouchable by the American government.

This would be the week that he was certain his enemies would remember. The only thing was that sometimes things don't always go as planned. True, his enemies would remember this day, but for very unexpected reasons.

I'll get Bone Neck, Fay, and Wyan Wyan all in due time, he thought to himself solemnly. It had to be done right. For Geno. Earlier this week, Geno had died. No funeral was given. The body was shipped to relatives that no one knew of. The news made all of 5th Street rejoice. The rest of the streets wept. Not Monster, though. he knew better than to weep. Soon, however, rather Monster knew it or not, 5th Street would rejoice even more and the streets would weep even more.

Monster gave ten bricks to his young niggas so they could get right. He also gave them his connects. he fitted T.Y. and Day Day with one of his mansions that he kept and gave them five million each. Monster had his plan. Get revenge and then retire. It was fool proof. However, death comes unexpected and you may not always die by the gun that you choose to live by.

"Fuck, fuck, fuck!" Monster screamed. "It's too fucking hot!" He was trying to find a way out of his burning condo in downtown Philly.

The fire seemed to cover all escapes. The thick smoke was dark and choking. It's haze clouded over the interior like the trail of a deadly ghost, its fumes were murderous and noxious. He could barely breathe. The conflagration seemed to cover all escapes. No front door access. No backdoor access. And the living room was connected to the fire escape. However, his living room was the source of the fervent heat that was burning the place down.

After gearing up for a run through the flames blocking his path, he took off at a dead run, hoping to break through the other side of the fire and reach the open window in the living room at the other end. The oxygen that it let in was a deadly burst to the flame, but it was, at the same time, life restoring and precious air. It fuels the flame, yet provides escape. "One...two...three!"

EYES WATERY, BLURRY FROM THE SEEMING ABYSS OF BLACK SMOKE. THE HEAT SEETHING, AND TEMPERATURE SOARING. CAN'T SEE SHIT. CAN BARELY BREATHE. LUNGS FILLING WITH CARBON

GASSES. SINGING THE ORGANS IN HIS CHEST. SKIN ON FIRE. OR IS IT? HEAT WAVES, MAKING THE ENTIRE PLACE LOOK LIKE A MIRAGE SWAYING UNDER THE INTENSE GAZE OF THE FIRES WATCHFUL EYE. BUT THIS IS NO IMAGE. THE FLAMES ARE REAL. WHAT HEAT! THE SMOKE IS REAL. AND DEATH. FOR, EACH IS A PLAIPORM TO THE NEXT. AND THE LAST... THE HIGHEST, YET THE LOWEST AT THE SAME TIME... IS THE END.

"Wyan! Bone Neck! Get in here, y'all" Fay called out at the top of her lungs. She was idle in front of the television set at Bone Neck's crib, their holdout for the past week, in fear for their lives. Well, in fear for THEIR lives, Fay thought matter-of-factly. He doesn't know about me, so I'm good, she conspired inwardly.

What, girl? I don't give a fuck about no fuckin' fire, bitch! I'm..." "Shut, and listen, nigga," Bone Neck said, cutting Wyan Wyan off so that he could hear the news anchor giving the story's details.

...Once again, we're here live on the scene, Channel Six News. Your source. Folks, there is a raging fire here burning this high priced downtown area condo to ash and cinders. This is the home and property of a very successful and prominent businessman. I've been told the body lust taken away was the home owner and entrepreneur by the name of Earl Moore. Young and very. very wealthy. folks. Our condolences go out to..."

Bone Neck broke in. "Yeahh! Yeah Bul. its over! The street is us yo! Heil yeah!" Bone was elated with the news.

"Damn. lust like that - huh?" Wyan said perplexed.

Somewhat disappointed. "Too easy."

Fay merely smiled and said. "Dummy should have given up the money. We could've finished him of quicker."

"Shut up. trick!" Wyan Wyan said. "We want some pussy." he finished.

"Yes. daddy." Fay responded and tended to the needs of Bone and Wyan.

CHAPTER 23

ONLY 1 ON TOP

The streets went berserk. Monster's death caused havoc and every single clique wanted a piece of 7th Street's respect. Day Day and T.Y. were officially "OUT." They had promised Monster before his death to live off the income of the Onyx Club, which was more than enough. Toby was holding down the strip though. He was a strong leader and was just as ruthless as T.Y. He had a ways to go before he could achieve status like Day Day, Geno, or Monster, but he was putting his thing down, hard on 7th McKean Street.

The only niggas they had constant beef with was 5th Street. Toby had successfully uprooted every other set. He was on top of a small army that Monster had built. Many of his men were loyal because of Monster and would remain that way because of him, come hell or high water.

The two young cats with the federal cases from the Bone Neck debacle ended up getting out on a technicality. They were back and were heading up certain blocks that 7th Street ran.

They would never forget what Monster did for them. The whole strip held a candle light vigil for him. there was close to three hundred people on Mercy Street that night. Then, everyone with a gun, virtually every single person there, let off a fully loaded clip in respect to this great goon gangsta named MONSTER. The city had been devastated. There were certain others who weren't so depressed, however.

5th Street was popping bottle every-night. Their money and power would increase. That's all that they cared about. The increase. Every other clique except 7th Street followed after 5th street. Even though 7th Street was larger than all the others put together, they still wanted to test. there was much ill will and blood shed during this war but Toby held his composure. He was smart and was doing his best. His men were always ready. He didn't have millions at his disposal like Monster did, but neither did 5th Street: The Enterprise, as they were called now. And that fact by its very nature, put them on even footing.

The loyalty, man power, and connects that Monster left behind gave 7th Street a slight edge. Their youth and inexperience hindered them because 5th Street Enterprise had Bone Neck and he was smart and was also a seasoned vet.

Tonight was Saturday. Hot Saturdays at Onyx. "Shit is popping, hoes and bottles!" T.Y. exclaimed from the owners VIP section. He and Day Day were chilling, watching the action.

T.Y. had moved up to a Bentley Coup and all kinds of dumb ice on his body. His necks was laced with platinum and diamonds and his wrist, fingers, and ears seemed to compete to see which could bling hardest. It was pretty much the same with Day Day. both of them enjoyed the lime light and the rich life that they were living.

It was a typical Saturday night. The club was jumping with niggas. Of course 7th Street still dominated here. T.Y. and Day Day were as loyal as they could be without getting into gang disputes because they had promised Monster before his death. They really wanted to step in and help Toby. They knew if they put in their help, that 7th Street would thrive; very near the level that it had with Monster at it's helm, but they couldn't go back on their word. In 7th Street, your word was your bond. Monster Geno, and Day Day used to kill niggas for them breaking their word to them. It was the most valued aspect of the group. Now it was his turn to keep his word and solidify that bond. And he would.

T.Y. was smiling like a clown and Day Day asked him, "What the fuck is wrong with you? Goofy ass nigga!"

T.Y. gestured with his hand to his lap and Day Day glanced under the table. There were two girls going bonkers on his dick underneath the table cloth's covering. "King Beef!" T.Y. said with a chuckle.

"Soft taco!" Day Day screamed with hysterical laughter.

"Oh, you got jokes, nigga? That was just one night. I drank too much, Day Day!" T.Y. rebelled, as he spoke about that night around three months before, when he and Day Day had a night out with two dime broads and T.Y. had too much to drink and couldn't get it up. That was about a month after Monster was gone.

Then T.Y. remembered Day Day's bad day, "Oh, don't think I forgot about you, limp noodle!" And they had cramps from laughing so much.

Everything was okay until the 5th Street niggas came in.

They hadn't been in the club since them niggas got that beat down and Herbie Luv Bug got knocked out by Day Day. Wyan Wyan got rocked by Monster as well that night.

It seemed as if time slowed and the music cut off as T.Y. and Day Day watched Wyan Wyan and Bone Neck walk in with an entourage. T.Y. grabbed his .50 cal and cocked it.

"Chill, T.Y. Remember our promise," Day Day said. They sat calmly in the other VIP section across the club and began staring over at Day Day and T.Y. intently. T.Y. and Day Day silently and slowly made a show of raising their weapons, cocking them and placing them on the table. "Just so them niggas don't think shit sweet," Day Day said.

"You think them niggas on it?" Wyan Wyan asked Bone Neck. "We ain't got no heat, nigga. They could chop us up right now. Easy. And get away with the shit," Wyan cried out.

"Man, bull, I told you a thousand times, the streets is saying that they gave Monster their word. Them niggas don't break their word. Ever," Bone Neck affirmed to him.

"You did," Wyan Wyan contended smugly.

"I ain't one of them," Bone Neck demanded.

Toby looked at Day Day and Day Day gestured back at him with a nod. Don't mean I have to be a part of it, Day Day thought innocently. "Watch this, Young T.Y.," Day Day said.

'CRASH!!!' Toby hit Wyan over the head with a champagne bottle and 7th Street began to pound the lights out of 5th Street. The bouncers chuckled as did Day Day and T.Y.

After a few minutes of chaos, Day Day signaled to security to get them niggas up out of there. "That shit was hilarious," T.Y. said. "Wyan looked like a crash dummy when Toby hit him with that bottle!" he finished with a smile.

Moments later, gunfire erupted outside of the club. 5th Street was shooting the club up. 7th Street began to swarm out to their cars and return fire. "Man, I'm sick of these niggas!" T.Y. yelled. "I'm bout to handle this shit, bull!"

"No, T.Y., we promised Monster that we wasn't going to kill them niggas without him," Day Day reasoned.

"Monster ain't here for that, now is he? He ain't here, so we gotta do it!" T.Y. professed.

"Nah, young'un. You an O.G. out of the clique now. You gotta set an example for the young niggas coming up. Even though we don't affiliate with them directly anymore, we still a part of them and they are a part of us, ya dig? They know the promise that we made. They gon' see it, Young T.Y. Stay strong. Don't you think I wanna murk them niggas, too? I been handling disrespectful niggas my whole life, and now I can't 'cause I made a promise? It ain't easy but we gotta do it. It's our word. Monster sees everything we do," Day Day said.

"I know, man, you right but them niggers is stone cold suckas is what they is," T.Y. rebelled.

"One day, bull. One day."

CHAPTER 24

OVERNIGHT CELEBRITY

"So, how did that shit happen?" T.Y. asked Day Day exasperatedly.

"Them niggas spirits is low. They scared and don't know what to do without Monster. They slowed down and eventually gave up," Day Day resounded. Anger flickering at the corners of his eyes and his words fuming with gasoline and venom.

"I'm saying, though, Day Day, them niggas was just whooping ass in the club last month. Bout like thirty damn days ago! You telling me that them niggas gave up just like that?" T.Y. asked curiously.

"Just like that," Day Day explained with even more hostility behind his voice.

"That's some bullshit, Day! Bullshit! I want parts. I want to help!"

"I know, T.Y., but you know our limits. We can't involve ourselves."

"So Fifth Street just run the streets now? Huh? Is you fucking kidding me? This shit is stupid! Them niggas is stupid!"

"Yup, them niggas is wiped out, Wyan Wyan," Bone Neck said puffing on a blunt. "Only, what? six months after Monster kicked the bucket, and they folding like fresh laundry? I told you all this shit was going to work out," Bone Neck said emphatically.

"Yeah, we did it, bull!" Wyan Wyan exclaimed in a drunken stupor.

"Nigga, you wasted!" Bone Neck laughed.

"So, bull, I'm straight. Just a lil' bit fucked up. That's all," Wyan Wyan smiled at his last words for no apparent reason as he and bone Neck laughed until their insides hurt.

"Y'all niggas is stupid," Fay said as she walked into the room. "Let me hit that, Bone," she said.

"No thanks, tramp, you suck wee-wee! Ewwww!" Bone Neck screamed as he and Wyan howled and doubled over with hysteria.

"Fuck y'all, I'll twist my own," Fay said as she stomped off.

I don't know how I got myself into this. These niggas promised me a couple million to just go along with this shit. Damn, I fucked up. I'm broke and these niggas is paid. I should of stayed with Monster. Oh well, he gone now. I had to move to the hottest new shit out. I ain't got no time for love. Only the love of money. Hey! she cheered herself.

There was a knock at the door. And then Bone Neck calling her name. There were about ten niggas in the living room sitting down looking at her. Bone spoke up. "We celebrating our takeover. And we are in dire need of your sexual expertise. Be kind and teach these gentlemen about the lip lock," Bone Neck said in a fake British accent.

"Yes, daddy," she said as she undressed. The love of money, girl, she told herself. It's worth it, right?

"Toby, what the fuck, nigga? We can't quit, man. Them 5th Street niggas is soft.as Gramma Cookies," the young nigga Funk said.

"I know, bull, but these niggas don't wanna fight no more. What I'm supposed to do about that?" Toby answered.

"Gear these muthafuckas up! Monster was on this shit, nigga. Ride or die for Seventh Street, nigga. 'You don't fight, you don't eat. And we respected the nigga because he fought, too. Just like you do, Toby, but you gotta get these niggas together, bull. We can't lose the streets!" Funk fired off. Man, we need Day Day and T.Y. to help us. What? them niggas scared or soemthing? They can turn this shit around," Funk declared.

"Nah, they ain't scared, bull! You sound like a fucking crackhead right now. You know who you talking about, nigga? Niggas die for talking that way!"

"My bad, Toby, you right," he said apologizing.

"Fuck it, it's cool. They can't participate in nothing that got to do with us. They promised Monster and they keeping their, word. O.G. promise, nigga. They under Seventh Street Law. So even if they was trying to be loyal and help us, it would be even more disloyal to go back on that. I wouldn't want that on my hands, their, disrespect, I mean. You can't disrespect Monster while he dead, nigga. That's bad karma or some shit," Toby finished.

"Yeah, I feel that," Funk answered. "So what we gonna do? We gotta do something," Funk said.

"Pray for a miracle, bull. That's what. Pray for a miracle."

CHAPTER 25

FAMILIAR MONSTERS

In the ninth month after Monster's death, Day Day got a phone call. "What's up?... Ay, what's popping, my nigga?... I been waiting on hearing from you. Yeah, Fifth Street The Enterprise is what they are called now. They run the streets. Been running them for about three months. Just the way you want it, huh? Yeah, me too. Aiight. Peace," Day Day responded with a smile as he hung up the phone. He couldn't wait to tell T.Y. as he picked up for another call.

"Yo, T.Y. What's good, but?... Oh, word? Sit down, I'm bout to fuck your world up, you ready?"

That Friday, Seventh Street had a meeting. There were close to three hundred people there. All of their spirits were renewed for war. Rejuvenated by the words that they heard. All they had to do was wait on the call from Day Day and it was on. Just a couple of more days. The call came. Now, it was time.

Wyan and Bone Neck owned a club on Market, Street downtown. They did excellent on Fridays. This Friday would not be so excellent, however. After they were sure the club was filled, about fifty niggas from Seventh Street charged the clubs front door and sprayed it until it looked like Swiss cheese. They laid everything down. It was a literal massacre. 42 people died. 36 of them were affiliated directly with 5th Street Enterprise, the rest were Seventh Street. "Casualites of war," Toby called them.

On Saturday every set that opposed 7th Street in the past was hit. And they were hit hard. Twenty-nine people died. Only one was from 7th Street.

Sunday morning, 7th Street got ruthless. They charged the police precinct. They stopped all movement. Seventeen dead badges. No one knew what was going on except 7th Street. There was a national security warning on t.v. for the area. This only made things worse. For the next week, people were being killed in broad daylight. In stores. At gasoline stations. In traffic. One nigga was in the delivery room with his girl giving birth and a "nurse" walked in and pulled a thunderous .40 cal from up under his smock and blew the new father's melon off. Then he pumped some rounds into the girl on the birthing table. The "nurse" just blended in with the crowd and escaped. Niggas was getting popped on the spot.

Fifteen 7th Street members were arrested for murder in one day. Thirteen for attempted murder. And another twenty-one were brought up on weapons charges. All forty-nine smiled in their mug shots. All declined to speak without an attorney present.

There were letters being delivered to the homes of rival bosses. They all read "Monster's Genocide. Welcome to another Monsters Ball!" The note meant death to a lot of people who read it. Those who understood it could not, however understand it. The Governorc called in the National Guard on the last day of Monster's Genocide. Everything calmed down until they left two days later. That was the shortest stint of martial law ever declared, but 7th Street did it to show their control over everything. They owned, the streets fully and no one knew who to blame for all of the murders, though there was speculation.

"So, tell me what the fuck happened!" Wyan Wyan screamed at Bone Neck.

"I don't know. It's like the world done went crazy or something," Bone Neck announced. "I ain't never seen nothing like it, Wyan. We can't leave, bull. Everybody dead. We all we got."

"Man, how them niggas just jump up like that? Where all that ammo and finance come from? It had to be Day Day and T.Y. They went back on their word."

"Yeah, they had to, Wyan."

"Fay!" Wyan called.

"What?" She called back.

"We hungry!" he shot back.

"And?" she retorted.

"Lazy ass bitch," Wyan grumbled to himself. Then all of a sudden, 'BOOM!' the front door splintered open.

"Oh shit," was all Bone Neck could muster before he was looking down the barrel of at least four guns. Bone Necks Wyan, and Fay sat on the couch looking as if they'd seen a ghost. When in fact they'd seen two.

"I burned down my own crib and used Herbie's body. It's simple. I had him on ice and he came in handy. I had Day Day come identify my ashy remains and sent Geno to South -Beach a week before me so he could begin therapy. I let the streets get word that he was dead. Easy. Only me, Day Day and Geno knew. T.Y. just found out," Monster said, smiling. "That's why my set went from docile to crazy in a heartbeat. They found out that I was alive, muhfuckas," Monster said before continuing. "I'm just back for a little revenge. I needed all that time because I wanted Geno well enough to have a hand in it as well."

"Yeah, bitches, muchfuckas shot me up, huh? Thought y'all killed of Geno, didn't you? Look at ya fucking faces. You should see yourselves," Geno chimed in.

Monster and Geno looked damned good for two dead men. Their physique had increased considerably, and they were darker from the Southern American sunshine. They ran the best and most lucrative whore houses even though it was highly illegal there. Millions of dollars was available to them and they were looking to capitalize as much as humanly possible. Monster continued.

"So, Day Day and T.Y. are leaving with us, say, in about four hours," Monster said, "Go ahead, Geno. Start shit off," he finished.

"Fay, I'm disappointed in you. Look at these niggas," Geno said, pointing to Bone Neck and Wyan Wyan. "And this is with 'whom you chose to place your faith?" he asked as he quoted Jay-Z, one of his favorite rappers.

Fay attempted to plead her case but was stopped short by Monster's right, fist before she could finish, or even begin for that matter. "Damn!" Wyan shouted.

She lost three teeth. As she was getting up off of the floor, dazed and bloodied, Geno spared no time and dumped four in her chest from his tailored .45 Colt 1911.

"Now you know she dead," T.Y. said solemnly.

"Y'all probably wondering who this is," Monster said as he

pointed to a massive man who stood near to six-foot-nine and weighed in at a bulky three hundred and fifty pounds. "His name is J-Bird. He don't speak much English but he knows his role. You fucked me! Both of y'all! Bone, especially you! So, now if its fuck me, then it gotta be fuck you. J-Bird, handle that," Monster said nodding at his huge German friend. J-Bird was a business partner and protector of Monster's interests. He was paid handsomely to keep his mouth shut, follow orders, and do what he loved doing anyway, since he washed out of the UFC for being overly violent; hurt people. J-Bird, on cue, snatched Bone Neck up bodily and carried him, wiggling and squirming like a wet fish, all the way to the back room.

It was ironic. In this room lie a dead girl, blood splattered all over the place and pooling around her body while from the rear of the place, you could hear clearly a man screaming as if he were a woman. High pitched, painful screams. Made a man want to cover his ears. Besides, Bird came with ten inches of limp dick. You could imagine what Bone Neck was going through. Or rather, what was going through him.

"Damn, he in there playing ping gong with his ass," T.Y. joked.

"Giving that nigga max pipe," Day Day said.

"Finish Him!" Monster imitated in a Mortal Kombat voice.

"Damn, he in there blowing that nigga back out!" Geno said, damn near crying with laughter.

"I know one thing, J-Bird ain't sitting next to me on no plane," T.Y. professed as they all shared in on the laughter.

After nearly ten minutes J-Bird came out of the room covered in blood and completely naked.

"Whoa, muthafucka, put a lid on them shits!" Day Day broke

in as he turned his head and covered his eyes.

Everyone fell out crying tears of laughter while J-Bird stood there in all of his glory smiling a near to toothless grin from ear to ear. He resembled a bird, albeit a large one, so that was how he got the nickname. Monster doubted that Jansen Wvladkowski could even understand where the name had come from, but one thing he understood very well, and was extremely good at: causing pain. "More," J-Bird said, smile not diminishing a centimeter. His voice was like gravel being poured over hot tar, his appearance was that of a naked murderer from some horrific psychopathic movie. He fit the role perfectly. Snatching up a crying Wyan Wyan, he trucked to the back with him tossed over his shoulder, slung like a sack of grain, and just as helpless, too.

It didn't take long before J-Bird brought Wyan Wyan's lifeless body back out; maybe two minutes and threw him on the floor. "No like," J-Bird said voicing his obvious displeasure with the offering. It was apparent that Wyan's neck had been snapped if the awkward angle of his head's positioning were any give away. Broken. viciously.

Geno, Day Day, T.Y. and Monster all stood there motionless, in intense silence, looking at the rag doll that Wyan had become. It was his just due, there was no doubting that, and no one would try, but the grisly scene was encapsulating. One needed to have a strong stomach to be able to see a man as dead as this laying at the feet of this behemoth of a man who stood in the middle of the floor smiling with blood and gore all over him, two men likely dead at his bare hands in less than 15 minutes, and a dead girl whose blood had soaked into the carpet and was still cascading down the walls from the violent impact of the bullets tearing through her tiny figure.

"Here, you can have this, Monster," T.Y. said.

"What?" Monster asked quizzically. "Have what, nigga?"

"These," T.Y. said as if it were obvious, holding out his hands although it was not difficult to see that they were empty.

"What the fuck is wrong with you T.Y. Ain't shit in your hands. What are you talking about? These" what?"

"Thheeeessseee nuuuutttssss!" T.Y. yelled and sprang away with maddening laughter as Monster tried to wrangle him.

All of them began laughing again, nearly crying and doubling over with hysteria. Even J-Bird joined in, though he was likely laughing at he knew not what, it was still funny. Well... they all had strong stomachs. Obviously. They ended up walking out of the door laughing... laughing... all the way to the bank.

EPILOGUE

OF THINGS TO COME

As T.Y., Day Day, and Geno sat in the room alongside Monster, the lights were dim and the sounds from the approaching sirens were becoming deafening. There had to be a million cops coming. They could barely hear each other. Day Day was bleeding badly from a bullet wound in his abdomen. Still, he angled a pretty Carbine Rifle out of the window and jacked off shot after shot from the fully automatic weapon as he tried with all of his concentration to murder a cop or ten.

Monster was letting off rounds from an M16. T.Y. ducked just as a bullet passed through his cabin window. What seemed like thousands of rounds were being fired between the two sides. Somebody was yelling something...

"See, I told you not to fuck with that bitch!"

"We ain't looking too good!" somebody else screamed.

That's when the explosion happened. It was unannounced. Unexpected. Unavoidable. And murderous. When it hit, it killed him... just like that, he was dead. The other three couldn't believe it. Pain and anger flooded each living face and heart.

But he would not be the only one to die. This is what it all came to. Life always ended this way... in death. Check out Monster II for more...

ITS BONE CRUSHER, BITCH!!!

ABOUT THE AUTHOR

Monster

Sept 2, 2020

12:43 p.m.

Interview with Earl Moore

This is an exclusive interview by Made Men Inc. with author, Earl Moore. Michael Woody sits down with Mr. Moore to pick his brain to learn what inspires him to write but more importantly to learn how had 7th st. located in South Philly, influenced him to become the man he is today. This unique interview is taking place at an extraordinary time in our country during a global pandemic, and a social revolution, inside the visiting hall of a federal institution. The interview that almost didn't happen.- M.W.

MM: The first question I have to ask and what I'm certain readers want to know is, what's it like to grow up on 7th st? Explain to those out there that will read this, who never been to philly. What is the atmosphere like on 7th st?

EM: It's rough. But we into fashion, getting money. Some of the livest niggas and bitches from 7th st. we like a small family which is why its not that much shooting around 7th st. There's no fighting and beefin, but if you get caught slippin you can lose your life around 7th st. them goons are there, You know? We on money though. Seven Street is like a baby New York. It's always something going on down there... It's the place to be.

We really don't consider ourselves as South Philly. Our old heads instilled in us the hustle. But when do we go to war with other neighborhoods 7th st go hard and put that work in... like I mention earlier its really no inner beef on 7th st we about that money, everybody happy around 7th st even the smokers are happy.

MM: How did you end up with a 30-year sentence in the feds?

169

EM: My connect set me up.

MM: How does that happen?

EM: He must've been gotten knocked on something and he gave up the people he was supplying and his connect.

MM: Who are some of the people you look up to?

EM: A lot of people inspire me but 7th st made me, because that's all I know.

MM: In a time like we're living in now and you, yourself having now been incarcerated for 13 years. What do you want the world to know about Earl Moore? What message do you have for 7th st?

EM: Learn from my mistakes and your mistakes. Y'all don't have to end up where I am now. Be Careful!

MM: Where do your motivation and consistency to write come from?

EM: WELL, me being in the hole/shu (Segregated Housing Unit) with nothing to do for six months and two weeks. I use to write my female friends, cussing them dizzy bitches out. I got tired of that shit... them bitches wasn't responding, then one day something dawned on me. When I was in juvenile detention... I was interested in writing stories, but my educational level wasn't there, but I always use to tell the neighborhood stories... I just didn't know how to put it on paper. So one day I just started writing down a lot of things, about things that was going on in my mind, the things I seen and experienced in my neighborhood then one day I looked up and I had about 400 pages front and back.

Then I had the chance to read rapper Earl Simmons (DMX) book and seen that he been through a lot of shit that I been through, but he was smoking crack. I wasn't doing that shit... niggaz from 7th st don't get down like that!

I was a hustler not a smoker. I don't get high. I don't even smoke cigarettes. I get high off money and bitches. But I felt like DMX's pain because he grew up without my father in my life. I was in foster care. I had to live with my grandmother at one point because my mother was running the streets. I was in and out of foster care but by the time I turned twelve I hit 7th st and that's all she wrote.

MM: When the offer was made to sell the rights to your book. What made you decline the offer?

EM: It wasn't about money for me. It was about doing something positive after sitting in that SHU for half of a year. Basically, I just wanted to make the best of a bad situation. I wanted to show my kids that you can turn a bad situation into a positive one and everything isn't about money. My first book has been out for a year now. I haven't seen any of that money... My sons Mother collects that money.

MM: What's your end game? You know... What's the goal? What is all this for?

EM: Shit... the end game? Its always an end game! Getting the fuck out of this prison! The end game... When I get out of prison, I hope I can continue to keep writing because that's what I like to do.

We Help You Self-Publish Your Book

**You're The Publisher and We're Your Legs.
We Offer Editing For An Extra Fee, and Highly
Suggest It, If Waved, We Print What You Submit!**

Crystell Publications is not your publisher, but we will
help you self-publish your own novel.

Don't have all your money? .... No Problem!
Ask About our Payment Plans
Crystal Perkins, MHR
Essence Magazine Bestseller
We Give You Books!
PO BOX 8044 / Edmond – OK 73083
www.crystalstell.com
(405) 414-3991

Plan 1-A 190 - 250 pgs. $719.00   Plan 1-B 150 -180 pgs. $674.00

Plan 1-C 70 - 145pgs $625.00

2 (Publisher/Printer) Proofs, Correspondence, 3 books, Manuscript Scan and Conversion, Typeset, Masters, Custom Cover, ISBN, Promo in Mink, 2 issues of Mink Magazine, Consultation, POD uploads. 1 Week of E-blast to a reading population of over 5000 readers, book clubs, and bookstores, The Authors Guide to Understanding The POD, and writing Tips, and a review snippet along with a professional query letter will be sent to our top 4 distributors in an attempt to have your book shelved in their bookstores or distributed to potential book vendors. After the query is sent, if interested in your book, distributors will contact you or your outside rep to discuss shipment of books, and fees.

Plan 2-A 190 - 250 pgs. $645.00   Plan 2-B 150 -180 pgs. $600.00

Plan 2-C 70 - 145pgs $550.00

1 Printer Proof, Correspondence, 3 books, Manuscript Scan and Conversion, Typeset, Masters, Custom Cover, ISBN, Promo in Mink, 1 issue of Mink Magazine, Consultation, POD upload.